The Exopotamia Manuscript

by
Maxim Jakubowski

BLACK
SHUCK
BOOKS

The Exopotamia Manuscript

First published in Great Britain in 2024 by Black Shuck Books

All content © Maxim Jakubowski 2024

Cover design by WHITEspace
from "The Hanged Man in the Forge"
by Félicien Rops
Courtesy of the Cleveland Museum of Art

Set in Caslon by WHITEspace
www.white-space.uk

The moral rights of the author has been asserted in accordance with the Copyright, Designs and Patents Act, 1988.
All rights reserved. No part of this publication may be reproduced or transmitted in any form or by any means, electronic or mechanical, including photocopy, recording, or any information storage and retrieval system, without permission in writing from the publisher.
This book is a work of fiction. Names, characters, businesses, organisations, places and events are either the product of the author's imagination or are used fictitiously. Any resemblance to actual persons, living or dead, events or locales is entirely coincidental.

978-1-917173-00-1

The Ways of the World

He came for the clam chowder and left the diner with the waitress.

Joseph Modiano was a man haunted by death.

Ever since he had lost his wife to dementia, he had been travelling through life without an anchor. In outward appearance, he was much the same as before, but inside, he oscillated wildly between grief and loneliness. Bearing a mental suitcase full of mounting regrets. Friends, as a way of complimenting him, remarked that he seemed to never age, but he knew they were sorely mistaken.

He could feel the years he had left racing by. His eyesight was beginning to fail; his teeth were in a bad condition, and he had lost two in the past eighteen months; he occasionally experienced strong muscular spasms in his left leg at odd times that made him want to scream, and woke up to five times a night to go pee. Worrying irregular pains in his knees and hips. A feeling that the writing was finally appearing on the wall.

When reading his daily newspaper, he would always head straight to the obituary page, hoping against hope it wouldn't again feature people he had known, or other minor personalities who happened to have been younger than him. His way of counting the days down to his own inevitable mortality. He just hoped it would, when the day came, happen quickly and he wouldn't suffer or be forced to navigate excruciating physical pain and anguish.

In the meantime, he travelled.

A lot.

To places he and D had been to, which always caused his heart to stutter; to new cities or landscapes he was curious about and that they had not managed to visit in the time they had been together and, he felt in retrospect, not made the most of.

He sailed off the coast of Nova Scotia, walked Water and Duckworth Streets in Halifax, navigating the beggars, the cannabis stores, the Dildo Brewery and Fat Bastard Tacos; he cautiously navigated the ice-strewn byways of Reykjavik, visiting the Penis Museum; ambled through the cobbled alleyways of Montreal and Québec City; he watched hardy surfers fight the mighty waves off Bondi Beach and roamed the streets of Paris, New York and Amsterdam unendingly in search of both memories and he knew not what. Sometimes a place he had almost forgotten would fortuitously be one they had strolled through together, and the dredged up memories would bring tears to his eyes while his heart tumbled into that familiar but awful pit of despondency.

In his callow youth, he had once written a novel in which the obviously autobiographical protagonist travelled the world in search of the truth, love and all that jazz. It was never published. Not only had he not yet lived properly or stored enough in the way of experiences, but his evocations of places foreign stemmed in their entirety from books and films and were utterly superficial. He had always been something of a romantic, but in unfocused ways. Had romance smacked him in the face, he wouldn't have known what to do about it.

So why was he now travelling so much? Solo cruises, beach holidays, city breaks. Indulging in nostalgia, a sliver of hope against hope maybe at the back of his mind about a final fling, a redemptive love affair? All of that and more. And filling the days until he would inevitably die, trying to make some sense of his life and the little he thought he had achieved, all the things he should have done and said better. Was he in his detached manner trying to keep ahead of the inevitable, or even the Devil?

Eventually, he realised, he would run out of places, destinations, ports in the storm.

An old Hávamál Viking proverb said that 'He is truly wise who has travelled far and knows the ways of the world.' In truth and depression, he felt he knew nothing.

The ship was on a 42-day cruise advertised as 'the rugged beauty of Iceland, Greenland and Canada in the autumn', but the weather had decided differently and a hurricane off the coast of Greenland saw the captain diverting the ship to Newfoundland, where they found shelter in the harbour at St John's for three whole days before being safe to venture out to sea again. He wouldn't see Greenland before he died, but he could live with that.

There are limited options in St John's and a sojourn of three full days can stretch the imagination if you are not a fan of raucous Irish bars or have already become familiar with the pale features of the half dozen beggars and junkies rooted to their regular patches on the main strip that ran parallel to the docks. To compound matters the town only had a single bookstore, with a limited selection unless you were a collector of vintage Canadiana, although he did come upon a reasonably priced first edition of a relatively rare Karen Blixen short story collection. He had never collected Blixen, nor even read her work previously, but the volume still had its original dustjacket and featured pretty black and white illustrations that reminded him of wood carvings. Joe always argued with his daughter that he was a collector, but she insisted he was more of a book hoarder, and it was true that he could hardly resist acquiring new books as if he had a moral duty to never leave a bookstore without at least a single purchase. And as much as he enjoyed his travels, insofar as he had a limited capacity for joy, he did miss his library badly when away from his sprawling London house.

The food on the ship was more than decent but Joe felt that, being in a port with a surfeit of spare time, it would make sense to sample the local seafood, and ventured offboard. There was a light drizzle falling as midday neared and the streets were sparsely populated. He wondered where everyone was: working, hiding, sleeping? Similarly, the first two restaurants and bars that he had spotted on the previous day were now closed and only appeared to open in the evening, so he strolled further down the main road, past the local Dollarama store, and took a turn to left, back towards the seafront, where a large luxury hotel stood. He had noted its presence and assumed it would have a dining room in operation. Not so. It, also, only opened in the evenings on weekdays. Joe sighed, more out of frustration than hunger. He had, on leaving the ship, set his mind on having oysters. Surely, this was the ideal place to sample oysters, on the North Atlantic shore and all that?

He then recalled a small diner he had walked by on his first day here, still on the main thoroughfare, but in the opposite direction to the mooring he had disembarked from, where many of the passengers and crew had congregated as free Wi-Fi was on offer. He'd casually perused the menu in the window out of curiosity and knew they had no oysters but remembered that, despite it being more of a breakfast place, they did have clam chowder listed, alongside the more commonplace fare of eggs, bacon, burgers and such. That would do.

He pushed the door open and a fragrant smell of coffee swept across his face, welcoming him inside; his glasses misted up and as he took them off to wipe them clean, a tall young woman, dressed in a black T-shirt and an equally black denim skirt that came to an abrupt end a full hand's length above her knees, greeted him. Did he want to use the bar or eat? On each side of the place's entrance were two separate rooms in which people were either drinking or eating, although most of them appeared to be busy on their phones.

"Are you still serving the clam chowder at this time of day?"

"Absolutely," she said, indicating the room to the right. "Come this way. Lily will be your waitress." She pointed him to a table by the window and stepped back, and he caught the sketchy outline of a blue-inked dragon unfurling all the way down her right leg. Another woman's voice said "I'll be with you in a minute" as he settled in his chair and briefly watched the waltz of waitresses and staff busily moving like worker ants across the diner's main area. They were all women, and every single one was dressed in black and, with no exception, each proudly sported at least one visible tattoo somewhere on her body; some he could see with his own eyes, while intuition suggested many others hidden behind the fabric of their differing black outfits. Was being inked a criterion for young ladies at the Water Inn?

"Good morning." A voice interrupted his mental speculation.

Joe was drawn to her voice but instinctively looked down at his watch. A Tissot on which he'd replaced the metal strap with a dark leather one to make it less ostentatious. It was already one in the afternoon. The waitress somehow realised her mistake and corrected herself. "Or, rather, good afternoon... I'm Lily, I'm your waitress today... Let me pour you some water and I'll let you have our menu... Coffee?"

He looked up at Lily.

She was shorter than the other waiting staff buzzing around frantically dispensing plates, cutlery, food and drinks, even though there were few customers. Naturally she also was dressed all in black but wore a pair of baggy trousers that flared down from her waist all the way to her Doc Martens. The sleeves of her dark T-shirt had been roughly scissored off at shoulder height and the side view of her small bra-less breasts inside it was inescapable. Her auburn hair was worn in a bob, there was a thin peninsula of freckles dotted across her cheeks and nose and her wide smile revealed glaring white teeth peering through heart-shaped lips. She couldn't have been older than mid-twenties.

Joe's mind froze. Lily kept on looking down at him, expecting an answer to her question. "Coffee?"

He took a hold of himself and finally responded "No coffee, thank you, but I will have a Coke with no ice, please." She had no visible tattoos, putting paid to his initial assumption.

"Coke no ice coming up." She handed him the menu and stepped away. He watched her retreat, sashaying towards the bar, a diminutive silhouette, all dark uniform and porcelain white skin.

She had made a strong impression on him, which he felt mildly embarrassed about. Was he becoming a dirty old man, perving on younger women now in his older incarnation? The sort of person he would once have held in terrible scorn? Led by his cock or a predatory imagination? Surely not. He could have argued he was just a proper admirer of beauty, but he knew he would be kidding himself. It was not the first time the sight of a pretty woman half his age had brought this sort of gentle lust to the surface. Just the way he was wired, he reckoned.

He was lost in thought when Lily the waitress returned.

"Have you made your choice?" she asked. One of her front teeth was ever so slightly crooked giving her smile a seductively asymmetric pattern of attraction. Her eyes were grey, the colour of a rainy day. He kept on staring at her, which didn't appear to bother her, as she stared back at him.

He took a hold of himself. "I'll go for the clam chowder, please."

"An excellent choice," Lily said. "What sort of bread do you want with it? We normally provide sourdough, but we have several other types."

"Sourdough will be fine," said Joe. He normally tore his bread, slice or roll, into small pieces and soaked them in the soup, so it didn't matter; although he was not normally a fan of sourdough, more of a white bread sort of guy.

"Excellent…" She hesitated, still staring quizzically at him instead of despatching his order to the nearby kitchen. "You're with the ship?"

"Yes, taking refuge from the storm out at sea. Captain Hugh said we should be here for three days in total; better safe than sorry."

"You didn't look local." She sketched a small smile. "But, I don't know, there's something familiar about you…"

"Not sure why, it's my first time in Newfoundland, let alone St John's…"

Lily nodded and moved away.

Ten minutes later, she brought his chowder. It was an enormous portion, which he welcomed, thick, creamy and piping hot, filling the deep bowl to the brim. He dropped the chunk of butter which came with the bread into it and stirred it in, watching the yellowish patterns it created as it melted, delaying his first sip of the soup only to appreciate it more once the combined flavours spread, caressing his tongue and palate. Joe liked his food. Since he had reached his 40s, his waistline liked it less. He would not miss oysters today, although a stray culinary thought sprang to mind of the time he had shamelessly consumed two dozen on the quay in Honfleur in France, just six months earlier on a market day, his paper plate perched on top a wooden barrel, struggling to detach the meat of the oyster from the shells with a fragile plastic fork and knife. It was curious how the taste of oysters could differ depending on where you ate them; each variety and locale different, from Boston to New

Orleans and all places in between. Some milky, some salty, some delicate, others aggressive in their salinity.

But the chowder warmed his guts nicely as the day deepened and he casually observed the comings and goings of the black-clad serving girls around the floor of the increasingly busy diner. He dunked a few extra chunks of bread into the creamy soup. Lily hadn't reappeared since she had served him. Maybe busy on the bar side of the joint? Or gone off shift? He hoped not; wanted to see her again, if only briefly at least when he offered to settle his bill, before he departed Newfoundland and she would become one of those hundreds of brief, tantalising memories he kept locked away, some of which still had the power to evoke joy. Although the majority did not, and triggered a painful form of anxiety instead. Which he had learned to live with. Unwillingly.

Joe spooned up the last dregs of his soup. Sighed. Pulled his napkin up, crumpled it on the table and looked around to catch the attention of one of the waitresses. He raised his hand discreetly and was seen by the initial waitress who had greeted him on entering the diner, guiding him to his table, the taller goth-like one with the mythical creature slinking all the way down her leg.

"Could I have the check, please?"

"No coffee?"

"No, thank you."

"Coming up."

A moment later, Lily reappeared and presented him with his bill. The meal had proven surprisingly cheap.

"Was it all satisfactory?"

"Absolutely."

He dug into his jacket pocket for his wallet and selected a credit card. Lily kept on gazing intently at him and then, as he handed the card over, and she read out his name, her eyes lit up.

"I knew I'd seen you before..." she muttered.

"Where?" Joe asked. Had they come across each other previously, he certainly would have remembered.

"You write books, don't you?"

"Hmm, yes... but I'm not that famous..." He could have counted on the fingers of one hand how many times someone had recognised him.

"There was a photo of you on the back cover of a book I read just a few weeks away. That's why you looked so familiar."

He was about to ask her which title it was. But she beat him to it. "The one about a woman who gives birth to tattoos when she..." Lily fell silent, reluctant to complete the sentence in public. Joe understood why.

He grinned. "Guilty as charged," he admitted. "One of my more... particular... books."

She smiled broadly at him, complicit. He even noticed her blushing slightly, her pale cheeks imperceptibly navigating from white to a barely-there shade of pink. But there was a sparkle in her eyes. Mischief rather than embarrassment. This encouraged him. "Of all the diners in Newfoundland, it was inevitable I should come here as all the waitresses appear to be sporting tattoos. Maybe it was fate and not the clam chowder?"

Lily was frozen in place, holding his credit card in one hand and the electronic reader in the other. She seemed amused. She finally swiped it and returned it to him.

"I've never met a real-life writer before."

"As you see we're totally normal in appearance." He was about to add 'like serial killers', but held the joke back.

Joe didn't want the conversation to end. He said the first thing that came to his mind, half-expecting the question would be answered by a slap in the face, well-knowing it totally inappropriate.

"So where is your tattoo, or do you have more than one? I can't help noticing there isn't one to be seen, unlike the majority of your colleagues here?"

Her flush deepened but she didn't lose her composure.

"Ah, but that's for me to know and you to discover…"

"So, there is one?"

She batted her eyelids in an expression of pretend innocence.

"Wouldn't you like to know?"

"That's not an invitation, is it?"

Joe felt they were like statues made out of salt, isolated in their own bubble inside the busy diner, immobile, flirting with fire as the rest of the world continued on its path around them.

Lily bit her lip. Looked down at the watch on her left wrist. "I finish my shift in twenty minutes. I'd love to talk more. Never met a writer before."

"I'd love that." He knew how wrong it all was. She was less than half his age, and there were a thousand reasons and counting not to take this a single step further. But how can you resist that miniscule glimmer of hope that burns inside your heart, mind or guts? Chance in a million and all that. At worst you'd just be another old fool falling for the same trap. One final chance at the prize.

"There's the Irish pub on the other side of the road. We can have a coffee or some drink there when I get off, no? It doesn't get busy until the evening, so we'll almost have the place to ourselves." Lily suggested.

He readily agreed.

So, technically speaking, he didn't actually leave the diner with the waitress, but no one is complaining, are they? It's called the art of fiction, and hey, there's a writer involved!

The Ways of Lily

Lily was not originally from Newfoundland, but from Chicoutimi in the far North of Quebec, a place of lakes, endless forests and harsh winters. But her parents had moved there from Vancouver to teach at the local university when she still a child of two, and she did not acquire a French-Canadian accent by osmosis as they always spoke English at home. Growing up, she had always been the odd girl out, preferring books to company or dolls, a head or more shorter than other kids of her age, her mind wandering freely like a migratory bird across imaginary countries, worlds she had read about on the printed page, characters who never existed but should have. She found dreams more interesting than reality. She was evasive when it came to explaining why she had moved to Newfoundland. Something about reading about the province in a book and being attracted to it, only to find it a severe disappointment and not at all what she had hoped for or expected, but she couldn't afford to move anywhere else for now.

"Books can be deceitful," Lily said.

And so are the people who write them, Joe was tempted to confess, tricksters all.

He found her an object of utter fascination.

Much to his surprise, the interest was two-way traffic. Rock musicians had groupies in tow and at their beck and call; had he fortuitously come across a woman who was the alpha and omega of a writer's wishful thinking in a Newfoundland diner?

Watching Lily's eyes light up, he sighed, cursing his bad luck at finally coming across her at his age; much too late, he knew. Ah, how fate teases us. Had J.D. Salinger and Philip Roth, wonderful old pervs that they were, been bothered though? He reckoned it could have been worse; he could have fallen for the almost anorexic Ukrainian violin player in the classical duo playing three sets daily in the ship's lounges. Younger women were now in the habit of catching his attention with suspicious ease and he didn't like this new-found weakness in his libido. He couldn't accept the fact he was becoming a silent dirty old man.

"So are tattoos a condition of employment at the diner?" he joked, trying to steer their conversation to a less intellectual and elevated level. Lily was so earnest and wonderfully idealistic, he felt. The attributes of youth, before disillusion set in. She had just confessed that she also wanted to write one day but was sensibly waiting until she had accumulated enough life experience.

"No, I think the owners just have a thing for goth-like girls and the ink often comes with the mindset. Maybe they think we're decorative?"

"What about you?"

"Me..." She rolled her eyes, then realised what Joe was asking her about. "Oh, I only have two. Small ones, nothing spectacular. In rather private places. You would ask that, wouldn't you, Mr. Writer who has thing for tats? Might I enquire if you have any yourself? Only fair to ask, no?" Her look was mischievous as she turned the tables on him.

"Actually no…" he admitted.

Lily laughed out loud. "You write about them, but you shy away from them in real life then; I'd call that cheating…"

"Guilty as charged of being a hypocrite."

He was expecting her to ask him a question about the notorious scene in that old book of his, but she didn't broach the subject. He had a standard answer to hand anyway, as to where he found his ideas, and normally responded by stating he acquired them wholesale from a factory outlet in South Nottinghamshire.

Since finding himself on his own, his only socialising had been professional and superficial and Joe was delighted with the way the conversation with Lily flowed, as if they had known each other for years and didn't come from altogether different worlds, let alone generations. The fact she was so easy on the eye helped.

She seemed reluctant to talk much about herself, preferring to converse about books, characters, the magic of the imagination. He, on the other hand, felt a compulsion to share emotions, stories about the places he had been on his travels, music he had heard, books he had read, movies he had seen; all the things he could no longer communicate properly about as a reluctant solo traveller. And Lily was a good listener. She, on the other hand, had not been many places outside of Canada. Disneyland, Universal, Niagara Falls and little else.

He was telling her about New Orleans and its many splendours as the weak autumn sun stumbled below the horizon outside, windows darkening and night advancing over St John's' main drag.

"Do you work an evening shift?" he asked her.
"Not today."
"Join me for dinner?"
"Sure."
"Do you like oysters?"
"Believe it or not, I've never tried them!"
"You'll either love them or hate them," he warned her, and suggested they walk over to the big hotel on the waterfront.

By midnight, she had revealed het tattoos to him.

He was sitting in a frayed wicker chair in her attic apartment in the north of town. An art deco lampshade housing a single bulb shed a warm light across the narrow room as she shed her clothes, the black baggy trousers slipping to the wooden floor to reveal thin, shapely legs and a delicate waistline. She wore no underwear. Her shapely arse had visibly never seen the sun, resplendent in its whiteness and the mathematical perfection of the angle of her curves. Joe held his breath. She twirled around for him with a gleeful smile painted across her face.

"There..." Lily pointed at her bare cunt.

Joe squinted and saw it.

A tiny rose, thin black stem and scarlet leaves, no larger than a thumbprint, marking the space above her vulva where the vertical line of her lips stood like a gate to untold secrets and treasures.

"It's beautiful," he said.

She pulled off her black T-shirt. Her small breasts stood high. Below her right breast was a thin inscription in a gothic font.

He peered closer. She took a step nearer to him.

A single word repeated three time in an elegant, cursive form of calligraphy. Hope. Hope. Hope.

"You are amazing," he said, his voice tight with emotion, as he realised he was about to embark on a path that would inevitably change what was left of his life.

"Come to the bedroom," Lily asked, pointing in that direction, now naked and pale, her breath irregular, no doubt as surprised as he was as to how they had reached this point; total strangers less than twelve hours ago and now here, about to become obscenely intimate.

I know it's wrong for a thousand reasons, Joe told himself. *But how can I turn this down? I would think of this moment and regret it every minute of the day if I don't follow her into that bedroom...*

There was a knot in his throat. Fear. The prospect of joy.

Decades ago he had written a novel set in Newfoundland which had turned out to be something of a mess and had fortunately never been published, because the publisher had gone bust before the book reached that stage. Something about a war involving the mining of phosphorus which, he had researched, was actually produced in Newfoundland.

And now he stood alone in a small garret in St John's about to bed a Newfie, as Lily liked to call herself.

Oh, well. But first things first.

"Lily?" He could feel the heat from her close body floating toward him, bearing a gentle fragrance of soap and citrus.

"Yes?"

"A word of warning. And I'll understand if it presents a problem..."

"What?"

"I'm an older man. I'll be honest... I'm no longer in the prime of my sexuality. Erections no longer come easy for me. I don't stay hard long. You should not take it personally. It's me, not you; absolutely."

Her smile broke through like a flood of kindness. "Who cares?" she said. "I'm happy to take the good along with the bad."

The first time he touched her was electric.

It had been more than two years since he'd felt a woman's skin against his, and the feeling was downright exhilarating. As if he had forgotten the sensation and his whole senses were being drawn back to life.

This time, he swore to himself, *I will not make the myriad mistakes that marred so many previous relationships. I will finally get it right. One last chance.*

Joe packed his suitcase and left the cruise ship before it finally departed into calmer waters the following day.

"Why me?" he had asked Lily after she had given up her job at the diner and taken up his invitation to travel with him to faraway places.

"Because you're a dreamer too. I like you; I will stay with you for a while, but don't fall in love with me," she warned him.

'For a while' would do.

He booked the flights. St John's Harbour to Toronto to Venice, Marco Polo.

Lily packed her suitcase. "What clothes should I take?" She was folding T-shirts, and hesitant to overburden herself with outfits she might not be able to wear. She'd Googled the city on the lagoon and knew that winter there could bring *acqua alta*, and that the weather might prove inclement.

"Just your favourite handbags and gladrags. Anyway, we can buy any new stuff you might need or fancy along the way. Travel light. No extra burdens."

Joe had never been an optimist by nature, considering the glass of life half empty at the best of times, and during the few days they spent together waiting for their flights to Italy, he spent an undue amount of time just gazing at Lily – dressed and, even more so, undressed – as if jotting down every image and configuration of flesh and curves and particularities in his memory, capturing the subtle geometry of her body, her quirky beauty like a fly in amber, already anticipating the days when she would inevitably be lost to him. As if a masochistic form of pain was an indispensable part and parcel of any pleasure in life he was allowed. A necessary building stone towards the joy he was striving for.

It was raining when they left Newfoundland and Labrador, and absolutely pouring down more than 24 hours later when they left the airport in Venice. By the time they reached their hotel, trouping through San Marco with their wheeled suitcases in tow, via a succession of arches, bridges and passageways, they were soaked to the skin and their inadequate shoes felt beyond repair.

The clerk at reception greeted them with a beady eye, then checked on his screen and apologised, assuring them that he would of course quickly get them a different room with separate beds, "for you and your daughter".

Joe was struck dumb and felt his face involuntarily redden. But Lily saved the day by brazening it out and advising the clerk they were not father and daughter. "Do we even look alike?" she asked him, with a broadening smile, finding the situation rather funny. It was the clerk's turn to blush. As they made their way to the lift, Joe could feel the eyes of all bystanders in the reception area drilling into the back of his head.

It was the following day that they came by accident upon the small bookshop in Cannaregio. They were looking for a restaurant off the beaten tourist track which Joe had been recommended by the concierge at the hotel, and were actually lost in a warren of canals and bridges, some of which led nowhere, and were about to make a U-turn and somehow orient themselves back to the Rialto and more familiar ground, if lesser local cuisine, when the shop appeared out of nowhere on the corner of a side street which seemed to lead to yet another church.

Libreria il Sogno. The bookstore of dreams. The patina of years washed across its wooden door and the green hue of the front window made the place look as if it hadn't changed in a century and belonged to another era altogether, straight out of a brown-stained, water-damaged photo album. Joe's first thought was of the fabled Barcelona bookshop from the novels of Carlos Ruiz Zafón. Dusk was falling but a single light bulb could be seen shining intermittently in the depths of the store. Joe and Lily looked at each other, on a similar wavelength. They had seen so many souvenir shops with ersatz Carnevale paraphernalia and Murano glass in their wanderings that this felt like more of a coincidence, a trace of the real Venice finally being revealed in extremis.

"We should go inside, see if you can find something for your collection," Lily suggested.

"It looks quaint, but I can't read much in Italian beyond the daily newspaper headlines…"

"Haven't some of your books been translated into Italian?'

"That was a long time ago. They would be long out of print by now."

"Well, this looks just like the sort of store that would still have old copies hanging around, no? Wouldn't it be a coincidence if we did find something of yours?"

A metal bell perched above the door rang as they pushed it open. Then came a deathly silence. They waited. "Oh, I like this smell of old books so much," Lily said. Volumes overflowed from shelves, balanced on a couple of rickety tables by the back wall, piles rising from the floor almost forbidding access to the next room. It felt to Joe as if he had been sent back in time to better days, when finding a book in a store was also a voyage of discovery. The only concession to modernity was a row of spotlights fixed on a rail in the ceiling, highlighting half a dozen particular shelves. Joe's attention was inevitably drawn to the spines of the books caught in the strong glare of the light, separating them from the rest of the stockholding which was buried in relative darkness. He didn't recognise any of the books. They all had titles, but no author names spelt out across the spine, nor publisher's colophon. Having spent decades working in book publishing, this anomaly intrigued him. *The Rabbi of Tallinn, The Girl from the Australian Gold Mine, The Jew of Constantinople, The Mage of New*

Orleans, *The Philosopher Who Thought She Could Fly*. All actually in English. None of the titles were at all familiar to him; which rarely happened. Intrigued, he tiptoed past the obstacle course of the unstable book piles to get a closer look, Lily silently following in his footsteps.

He was about to pull one of the books from the shelf, the Australian one, vaguely recalling a tale a friend of his had once related to him of walking out naked into a dust storm in a small Australian mining town, and how sexually turned on she had felt by the experience. He wasn't aware she had actually written the story. He was indulging his curiosity.

"Ah, visitors to the dream." A basso profundo voice startled them and they turned around. A man was standing there, appearing out of nowhere. He was tall and skinny, wearing a tweed three-piece suit in variations of beige. His face was unremarkable but his eyes had a piercing intensity. He looked familiar to Joe, who was unable to pinpoint why or where they might have crossed paths in the past.

"I was about to close for the day, but you are most welcome. I've been expecting your visit…"

"How come? We only came about your store by accident. Took a couple of wrong bridges and found ourselves here. Didn't even knew you existed," Lily stated.

"All true dreamers eventually find us," the bookshop owner pointed out. "The roads lead this way, and then to the forest, don't they?" He looked intently at Lily, ignoring Joe altogether, as if he and the young woman were accomplices, partners in some unspecified conspiracy. Joe felt a tremor of apprehension washing across him. Imagined for a brief moment that he was just a helpless character in a book written by a stranger, a puppet on invisible strings, his fate dictated by the *tap tap* of fingers on a keyboard. What forest? What the fuck? And why was Lily acting as if this encounter was all in a day's work?

"But I am being impolite," the tall man said. "Let me offer you a coffee and then I can guide you to the books you are seeking, Joseph. It is Joseph, no? And you are Lily?" There was no way he could have known their names. "Let me guess, cappuccino for the lady and a double espresso with lots of sugar for you?" He didn't hang around for an answer, instead swiftly navigating the books on the floor and the tables to disappear into the next room.

Joe was speechless. He was frantically trying to process what was happening and his eyes were again drawn to the same shelf he had perused with growing curiosity just a moment ago. A further English language title caught his attention. *The Mandrake Forest*. Coincidence?

"How the hell can he know our names?" Lily asked. "Did you set this up?"

"Absolutely not," Joe protested.

"This is spooky. I want to leave, Joe. I don't like this. Not at all."

"Shouldn't we wait for the coffees and then make our excuses?"

"No. Right now. I insist."

They noiselessly made their way back to the front door before the proprietor had an opportunity to return and stepped into the narrow street that abutted the canal. The waters were grey as night fell like a lazy cloak on Cannaregio. Again they got lost on the journey back to the San Marco area, despite the many signs, and didn't reach their hotel until late, going straight to bed without eating. Lily was visibly freaked out, angry and Joe couldn't find the words to appease her. It wasn't quite their first row, but not far off.

When Joe woke up the following morning, Lily was no longer in the room. He looked out for her in the breakfast salon downstairs but she nowhere to be seen. Maybe she had snacked earlier and gone for a walk, to clear her mind. He reckoned he should do the same and slipped his trainers on. The streets were empty in the dull early morning, and he soon realised he was heading towards Cannaregio, seeking possible answers to yesterday's curious incident.

He crossed the same bridges, walked by the churches until he found the corner where the bookstore had been situated. But it no longer was. The space was now occupied by a small bar. The mysterious shop had been called *Il Sogno* but Joe knew for sure he hadn't imagined it. He had been inside, seen the books, spoken to the owner, smelled its unique fragrance of old paper and dust. Gone. He tried to retain his composure, but a chill traversed his soul.

By the time he reached the hotel, crowds of tourists were already swarming down Venice's narrow streets. The moment he opened the door to their room, he knew that Lily had flown. Her suitcase was gone and the cupboards and drawers lay orphaned, leaving just his own badly-folded clothes, still carrying her fading fragrance from the brief time they had shared together.

The Ways of Venice

Joseph spent a further week in Venice. On his own, feeling sorry for himself. He moved to a smaller hotel, on the Lido, a boutique two-storeyed villa hidden behind a busy garden where the trees were in the process of shedding their leaves for the season, allowing intermittent light to brighten his room when the clouds obscured the cold sun outside. Streaks of white splashed against the blue-painted walls like a reversed Rorschach test pattern.

Neither the bookshop nor Lily reappeared.

The vaporetto turned the bend.

He'd witnessed it in countless paintings by Canaletto, Turner and others, a thousand and one photographs and movies and TV documentaries, but still the eternal view unfolded like a slow-motion epiphany.

The Grand Canal in all its majesty. *Canal Grande*.

Moving past the Ponte degli Scalzi, the choppy waters flowing all the way downstream toward the Rialto Bridge that loomed in the grey distance, the crumbling stone outposts on either shore like parallel rows of zombie guests at a wedding waiting for the bride and groom to troop past and be assaulted by clouds of confetti, the domes of churches in the hinterlands, the procession of palazzi straight from the pages of history and guidebooks: Gritti, Dona Balbi, Zen, Marcello Toderini, Calbo Crotta, Flangini, Giovanelli, and on and on, like a litany of open-mouthed operatic celebrations of decay and grandeur, the sound of water lapping in the wake of the vaporetto's passage, the unique smells of La Serenissima, gulls above observing his steady journey toward the open spaces of the lagoon, past the markets, and finally the Ponte dell'Accademia and onward, beyond Piazza San Marco and the Doge's Palace and into the murky emptiness that separated the core part of the city from the nearby islands.

It was not the first time he'd made this journey, but it always took his breath away as the façades unrolling on both sides of his field of vision steadily unveiled centuries of history. Of stories imagined and read about. Of classic movies. Of books. Stories that stick in your throat and in your mind like rough diamonds full of fury.

The hiccupping engine of the vaporetto guided him into open water past the final promontory of the Giudecca, beyond the tip of San Giorgio Maggiore, and cut through a cluster of lingering mist, heading for the fast-approaching line of the Lido.

Joe wrapped the black cashmere scarf tighter around his open collar as the marine breeze made its coldness felt. Looked around. Since the San Marco stop, there was just a handful of passengers left on the vaporetto. Mostly locals with bulging shopping bags, a couple of teenagers busy texting on pink cell phones, a well-dressed businessman of some sort whose hairpiece was an uncomfortable match for his russet moustache.

And sitting right at the back, lost in distant dreams of an unfathomable nature, the young woman. He'd distractedly noticed her boarding the vaporetto at the Santa Lucia train station, running down the stone steps toward the embarkation point, holding her bag in one hand, her golden hair flowing behind her. The water bus was just about to depart and she'd only caught it with a few seconds to spare. For a terribly brief moment he'd thought it might be Lily, but the hair colour and the height soon denied him that hope.

Her green mac was now unbuttoned, displaying the violent fire of a red sweatshirt over skinny black jeans. Even though, like him, she was obviously a tourist, she appeared different. As if she belonged here somehow, despite being a stranger, amongst the cold breeze of the lagoon.

And come to think of it, how did Joseph himself appear to onlookers? Yet another tourist with no luggage. A man with wild gray hair curling out of control, his stocky frame bulked up within a heavy brown leather coat. Middle-aged, unremarkable.

The vaporetto shuddered to a slow halt in front of the pier, and the passengers disembarked. Joe was in no hurry and allowed the locals to stream past him before he even rose from his wooden seat. As he stepped off onto the island, he had a final look at the receding water bus. The young woman who'd attracted his interest was no longer sitting in the rear, although he had somehow not noticed her overtaking him. Strange. He looked ahead at the small tree-lined piazza which hosted the vaporetto station. The other passengers were dispersing in two or three separate directions but there was no sign of her. He sighed and mentally speculated how tall she had actually been. Her posture had reminded him of Kathleen, who had been five feet eleven, lithe and clumsy and surprisingly submissive between the sheets. Joe sighed again as memories came streaming back in a torrent before he deliberately cut them off. Now was not the time.

He looked ahead. The piazza was empty, like a set for a ghost town in a movie. Shuttered cafés on both corners of the main road which, he recalled, led a few miles farther down to the beaches, the big hotels and casinos.

But somehow it now appeared so different, as if his memory was playing tricks on him and he hadn't actually been here before all those years before.

A car crossed the piazza in front of him at a low speed and it was something of a shock, a disconnect. You just don't expect cars in Venice. But he reminded himself this was the Lido and not Venice itself. A random thought occurred to him: Do they ship the cars in from somewhere? How?

Behind him the departing vaporetto shrunk in size, cutting through the waters, returning to Venice. Joe glanced around. A long road disappeared ahead, in all likelihood leading toward the Lungomare, he remembered. All roads south on the Lido invariably reach the Lungomare, the Adriatic.

He set off. Was it the second or third turn to the left? He tried both and was soon lost. Every small turn off the main road looked alike. Unable to find the hotel he was staying at again, he stumbled his way back to the main road. There was no one around he could ask for directions and he couldn't get a connection on his iPhone and search Google Maps to find his bearings or assist.

The cold breeze was insidiously finding its way through his heavy leather coat. He shivered as every bone in his body groaned.

"You took a wrong turn."

Joe swivelled around.

It was the young woman from the vaporetto. Out of nowhere.

He looked her straight in the eye. Green; almond-shaped. She held his stare, her painted Mona Lisa lips fixed in a semblance of irony.

"How would you know?" he queried.

"I know," she said.

"You've been here before? Do you live here?"

"I just know," she reiterated.

From the moment he had first heard her voice, he had been glued to the spot. He felt an ache in his right hip. Her eyes were hard as ice, deep wells of certainty.

"Okay," he said.

"Just follow me." The young woman's voice was transatlantic, impossible to pinpoint its origins with any degree of accuracy. She could as easily be British or American, or even from elsewhere, the words carefully modulated, or maybe the product of expensive elocution lessons.

She took a long, almost manly stride toward the curb and Joe trouped along behind her. Her hair shimmered in the winter breeze, curls sprouting in every direction like a crowd of thorns. He called out to her, "I'm Joe, by the way…"

She nodded, as if she already knew this.

"What is your name?" he persisted.

She turned her head around toward him and smiled gently, as if hesitant to reveal her true identity.

"My name hardly matters," she finally said, and increased her pace. They were now walking down a narrow tree-lined street of high brick walls and concealed gardens. It was all beginning to look familiar to Joe. He dug his gloved hands deep down into the pockets of his coat. How could it be so damn cold in Venice of all places? He'd somehow never associated the city with this sort of weather.

Her slim ankles danced ahead of him as she made her way through the narrow Lido backstreets.

"How did you know where I was staying?" Joe asked the perplexing woman as they finally arrived at his hotel. It was not the route he would have chosen, had he recalled the right one, but the destination was the same.

"Maybe I read it in a book..." her grin lit up her face.

He decided to play along.

"What book?"

"One you haven't written yet, maybe. You never found the courage to pick up any of the books on that shelf at the store the other day, did you?"

When they entered the grounds of the hotel, Joe immediately recognised the place. The overgrown gardens, the clean-cut façade. A feeling of déja vu. Like the story he had once penned, inspired by that gut-wrenching affair with Giulia, all of two decades ago, in which a tourist in Venice is seduced by a ghost who makes love to him but steals his life essence, and leaves him dead the following morning, an angel of death passing through *La Serenissima* collecting souls, or maybe something even more intimate. He hadn't realised when he had booked into the boutique hotel earlier in the week, how much it resembled the place he had invented in his story.

Joe was struck dumb. They walked side by side into the hotel. The exiguous lobby of Villa Stella was empty.

"Come," the young blonde woman beckoned him, as she lifted the oak panel that separated the granite-topped registration counter from the common area. She slid elegantly between the counter and a high-backed chair and turned to the wall where the room keys all hung, taking one. Maybe she was staying here too, which would explain her relaxed familiarity. But how could she have known it was this specific hotel he was seeking after the wrong turning he had taken? And where were the staff?

"It's out of season," she stated, as if in answer to Joe's unformulated question.

"And you just happen to have the run of the place?"

They walked up the stairs

"You could say that." An enigmatic smile slowly spread across her lips. She had cheekbones to kill for. They headed down the deep-carpeted corridor, reaching the last of the six rooms on the floor. She turned the key in the lock.

The room they stepped into was frozen in time, conjuring up too many memories and images sharp enough to puncture his heart and soul. Yes, Joe had been here before, but it was in a story he had written, in his imagination. That's why he recognised it. The art deco light fitting. The painting on the wall of Icarus falling from the sky. All of a sudden, he lost his resolve.

"Would you mind if we came back later? Have a walk first?" he enquired.

"No problem."

They took the main road toward the sea, where the thin strip of land of the island bordered on the

Adriatic. Turned right at the Lungomare, walked down Gabriele d'Annunzio where it turns into Guglielmo. All the while in deadly silence, a million and one thoughts swirling around in Joe's head.

The Hotel des Bains was shuttered and shielded by a barbwire fence. He had read somewhere it was soon to be remodeled into an apartment block. Its beach was also inaccessible, its golden sands lying wet and forlorn with scattered frayed deckchairs upturned here and there, like memories of a past, more opulent era.

"Sad, no?"

"Yes," Joe agreed.

"I've always wondered why Thomas Mann called his book *Death in Venice*. It should have been *Death on the Lido*, properly speaking."

"I know," Joe said. "Maybe it doesn't have the same ring. People always think of Venice first. The Lido just hasn't the same romantic connotations."

This was where Aschenbach had coveted the adolescent boy Tadzio and allowed death to welcome him into its arms in the novella. Joe hadn't actually read it, but he had seen the Visconti movie. Though he would never admit to this publicly. There were too many classics he hadn't actually read.

"I only saw the movie," the young woman said.

"Me too."

"Philistines, eh?"

"Absolutely," Joe said. They both laughed.

"Anyway," she continued, "Aschenbach died of cholera, not a broken heart. A fanciful notion, but quite unrealistic."

There was that characteristic spark of mischief in her eyes rising to the surface.

They continued down the road, walking parallel to the sea. The grey sky chilled his bones to the core. It looked as if it would soon begin raining. He tightened his black cashmere scarf around his neck.

They reached the Excelsior Hotel, which was also shuttered for the winter season. The main film screenings took place at festival time in the bowels of this luxury hotel.

"Did you know that Venice no longer has even a single cinema?" Joe told her. "A city that hosts one of the world's major film festivals doesn't even have a functioning movie house throughout the year. No demand. Not enough people. The population is steadily falling. Young people don't want to stay in Venice any longer. Tourists don't come here to see movies. They have other interests."

"Fascinating," the young woman replied. "So what do you think brings people here in such numbers?"

"The beauty of decay, the weight of history, I don't know. Maybe it's just habit, like lemmings. They reckon it's a place everyone has to see at least once in their lifetime. Before they die."

"I thought that was Naples."

"Both," Joe said. He'd never been to Naples. Nor even wanted to.

A gust of wind surged past him, moving between the sea and the lagoon. He shivered yet again.

"Can we turn back?" he asked her. "This is getting too cold for me. And at this time of year, all much too desolate." He pointed to the abandoned beaches and shuttered buildings.

"It's just winter, Lido winter" she remarked. And swivelled around.

He remembered how warm the hotel had felt earlier, even though it was empty.

They were back in the room she had commandeered.

"So what brought you to Venice? Did you come for the churches?" she asked him.

"No."

"Did you come to Venice for the canals and the art?"

"No."

"For the glass baubles from Murano, the food, the way the evanescent light plays on the slow-moving waters of the canals and the lagoon, the history, the gondolas, the teeming Rialto Bridge markets, the way the water slops against the stone walls of the canals when the tide rises…" A litany of questions.

"No, no, no…"

And Joe was too ashamed to tell her the truth; he hadn't the courage or the audacity to admit to her that the only reason he had returned to Venice was because a waitress half his age had suggested it as a reason to keep on sleeping with him, and he had found himself confronting his own history, his memories, to wallow in the past, to understand once and for all that some things will never be the same again whatever you say or do. To finally come to terms with the fact that Giulia had been his last great adventure. And there would be no other. As if life had provided him with x number of chances, and he had taken them all, run out of numbers.

But then, he guessed she knew all this already.

He was now sitting in the hotel room, half a buttock uncomfortably perched on a corner of the same bed in which he and Giulia had once made love in every conceivable position, while the blonde stranger from the vaporetto stood by the door, observing him in silence, a detached interrogator in the house of love.

"Do you even have a name?" he asked her.

"Do you want me to have one?"

"Yes, I do."

She paused for a moment. Pondered. Decided. "Make it Emma."

"Your real name?"

"Does it matter?"

"Not really, but this whole situation feels less awkward you having a name, I suppose."

"Makes sense, I agree," she nodded.

"Emma?"

"Yes?"

"Who are you and what the fuck do you want?"

"Admirably to the point."

"And about time too. So?"

"Joseph, you know who I am."

"I don't."

"Just another femme fatale in a story you are still writing."

"That doesn't make any bloody sense..."

"And no, I'm not about to fuck you and steal your soul, or your seed, or whatever the plot requires. I know about Lily..."

"Do you? Where is she? What's your connection to her?"

"Just characters, women, ciphers, misbegotten angels, creatures of the page. Surely you realise that?"

Joe knew she was deliberately teasing him but he could somehow see a larger pattern at play, something that was beyond his control. An underlying reason for all his travelling, his blind quest for whatever joy was left in the world.

He was beginning to feel drowsy.

He blinked. Once. Twice. His jaw loosened.

Deep down inside, he knew who Emma really was. And Lily. They were not accidents on his road to nowhere. Could it happen any other way?

Did he think they'd just arrive on the scene, knocking on the door like the long-expected killers in a Hemingway short story, or dressed in a red vinyl coat like the Venice-haunting dwarf in the movies?

And again, he asked himself, wasn't it right that Emma should be a sumptuous long-legged blonde, with tousled hair, emerald-green eyes, pale skin, and cheekbones to kill for? The saving grace of fate, or mere coincidence?

"What now?" Joe asked.

From the outer shores of dreamland, he thought he heard her say "Not yet, Joe. Your time is still to come, Joe. The forest is patient..."

Through the open curtains of the hotel room, he could see the evening darkness take hold of the sky and, beyond the Villa Stella's shrubbery, descend on the Lido. If he closed his eyes, he could imagine the pinpoint myriad lights across the lagoon illuminating the floating city. The thought occurred to him that he'd never been to Venice at *acqua alta* when the water surged across Piazza San Marco.

Sleep embraced him.

The vaporetto turned the bend.

The Ways of the Roots

When he woke the following morning, he found he was back in his own room. The mysterious woman who had called herself Emma was gone. The staff were present and on duty, busying themselves with their tasks for the new day, hoovering, cleaning, serving breakfast, the smell of coffee wafting through the lobby and the annex where the buffet was situated.

He was starving and ate copiously.

He was about to return to the room when, passing by the reception counter, he was hailed over by Marina, the assistant manager, a grey-haired woman with an aristocratic allure.

"Ah, Mr Joe... There is a letter for you..."

A thin white envelope posted in France, if he believed the stamp. The address and his name handwritten in spidery script. He was puzzled; no one knew he was staying here, let alone in Venice.

He opened the envelope back in his room, taking a deep breath, apprehensive.

It was from Lily, of all people.

There was something charming and childish about her thin scrawl, all in curves, every individual letter carefully crafted and connected to the next. He could almost imagine her writing it, the tip of her tongue studiously peering through her pink lips.

An apology. Some form of explanation.

How she was sorry to have abandoned him. That she was cowardly, she knew. At *Il Sogno*, while he was peering at the titles on the shelf, all those impossible books that made no sense, she had distractedly picked up another volume from one of the tables, shaken the dust from its anonymous cover and opened it to a random page, in which a character with her name was making love in a bedroom in the very same hotel they were staying at with a much older man whose unruly hair spilled wildly over his collar. It had spooked her to the core. So, she'd run away. She knew she shouldn't have. She was now in Paris, she wrote, and it would make her happy if he were willing to forgive her and come and join her there. There was a name of a hotel in the Latin Quarter.

As it happened, he knew Paris well. Had lived there for several years when he was younger.

But still, this turn of events did not make any sense. How could Lily know to send her note to the Villa Stella?

Of course, he would travel to Paris. For a second chance?

For an answer to the many questions that were now floating around in his mind like unexploded military ordinance? Because his cock was taking precedence on rational thought? He had always been a fool for lust, ready to jettison reason for the feel of a woman's bare skin, the sound of her voice, the heartbreaking depth of her eyes or the ever so subtle variations on the colour pink that an open cunt could provide and in the process steal his breath away.

Maybe Paris would prove warmer than Venice in winter? As good a motive as any, he reckoned, as he tried to justify his course of action to himself.

The Exopotamia Manuscript

The trumpet player wore a grey three-piece suit that looked as if it was one size too large on his skinny, almost emaciated frame. He was improvising on 'A Night in Tunisia', a tune by Dizzy Gillespie. Joe had never been much of a jazz fan, more of a rock'n roll sort of guy, but Lily had found a job serving drinks in this small club, in a cellar space near St Michel on the rue de la Huchette, and worked there evenings, so Joe had tagged along. A low cloud of cigarette smoke hung over the cramped room.

Since hooking up with him again, Lily had reverted to her customary insouciant self, but had been evasive when he had queried how she knew where to contact him in Venice, asserting he had actually left a forwarding address at the desk of the hotel where they had stayed together. A fact he had no memory whatsoever of.

"You know he writes books too?" Lily said to Joe, glancing at the trumpet player. "I heard people say they're good, slightly bizarre, but they're all in French, so no good to me."

The musician's hair was thin and receding, his nose sharp as a knife, and his cheekbones rose and fell with every successive note he drew out of his instrument.

Joe kept on staring at the stage.

"Maybe I can introduce you?"

She knew Joe was normally reluctant to talk about his past books. He was a writer in disguise, someone who hated the act of writing although he liked having written. It wasn't false modesty, just the fact he had nothing to say about his paltry literary accomplishments. Lily had learned early, while they were still in Newfoundland, not to pursue the subject.

"Does he speak English?"

"He does. Has even translated American pulp novels. He's sort of famous here. He's not a full-time musician; works for a record company, but also writes poetry and plays."

"A man for all seasons, eh? A multi-tasker, no less!"

Joe had not always wanted to be a writer himself. As a kid, his passion was for bicycles, and he had harboured dreams of racing in the Tour de France. Later, in his teenage years and well beyond, he dreamed of becoming a bass player in a rock and roll band. The only drawback being he couldn't read music, let alone play an instrument. In idle moments, he still had daydreams of unlikely musical glory, and often wondered how different his life would have turned out had he taken that fork in life's garden of countless paths.

The trumpet player had reached the end of his improvisational solo, and the piano player was now embarking on a lengthy detour of his own, while the rotund black drummer kept the rhythm going, his metronomic beat keeping the melody grounded.

Lily was circulating around the room now, taking drink orders, and Joe was sitting on his own. Stepping off the small circular stage, the trumpet player made his way towards the table where Joe was nursing a coffee.

"May I?"

His accent was strong; there was no mistaking he was French.

"Please."

"I'm Boris," he introduced himself.

"Joe."

"I know, the lovely Lily has told me about you. You are her man, no?"

"I suppose I am, if you put it that way." Her man! At least, she hadn't passed him off as her father or uncle...

"You write too?"

"I used to. It's been a long time since I've done anything new. Not sure I will. The ideas are just not there any longer; or the will... Running out of words."

"You will write again, I am sure. People like us they die at their keyboard, no? Best way to go."

"That's reassuring. So what sort of things do you write?" Joe asked Boris.

"It's difficult to say. Books that don't sell many copies is the only thing they have in common. Perverse love stories maybe..."

"Join the club."

"Lily, she says you are always writing about other women."

"Does she? But is there any subject that might be better to write about?"

Boris laughed out loud. "I like you."

"So what are you working on now?"

"It will be about a group of random people who meet up in the middle of a desert to build a railroad and then fall in love, fall out of love, all that jazz. But I think it's not enough of a story yet. Just a feeling. Not really a plot, a story."

"I'd read that."

"Thank you. I have a working title: 'Autumn in Peking'."

"You mean Bheizing?"

"No. Definitely Peking. But before I can spend time developing it, I have a commission to deliver. An American-style pulp novel, with lots of sex and violence. For the *Série Noire*. It will be under a pen name, though. But what about you, not even the kernel of an idea?"

Joe took his final sip of coffee. Boris offered him a cigarette, which he declined, then lit up his own. The trumpet player's face was surrounded by a halo of sharp tobacco smoke. He truly had no wish to give birth to any further books but, on the spur of the moment, he said "Maybe something about ghosts?"

"Ah, phantoms! That is interesting, it's not something I have ever done."

"Lately, I seem to be surrounded by ghosts, women, books, as if the fabric of the world is shifting around me," Joe confessed.

"Are these ghosts frightening?" Boris asked.

"Not really. More like disturbing, irrational..."

"And these ghosts, are they men or women?"

"Oh, always women. Absolutely..."

"Ah, lady ghosts, that sounds promising indeed," Boris opined.

"And somehow the ghosts appear linked in some incomprehensible manner to books. Real books, but ones that have never existed. I know it doesn't make much sense."

Lily was now between shifts and had joined them, sitting alongside Joe.

"I told Boris about that spooky bookstore in Venice and the damn book that scared the shit out of me, in which I seemed to be part of the story. Still feels like a dream. Or a nightmare..."

"Interesting," Boris furrowed his brow. "Do you remember the title, maybe?"

"I'm not sure," Lily said. "I was so shocked I didn't give it much attention. Maybe something about a forest... And, yes, Merlin... No, not that name, but similar." She scratched her cheek and swept her hair back from her face. Both men looked at her intently, as if hoping to draw the name out. She looked back at them blankly. The name wouldn't come. Boris rose. "My next set is coming up. I need a chat with the other musicians, have to agree about what tunes we will be playing..." He bowed, turned his back to them.

Lily almost shouted out the name she had dredged up through her layers of memory. "Mandrake, that's it... Mandrake."

Boris stopped.

"Fascinating..." he remarked. "We shall talk more later, OK?"

Joe's mind was in a complete whirl. "I saw another copy of that particular book on the shelf," he said. "I'm sure it was called 'The Mandrake Forest'..." It felt like assembling an enigmatic and highly complex jigsaw puzzle, but he was increasingly worried what the overall picture would turn out to be once it was eventually completed. A puzzle whose final image was still obscured from view and was being assembled one piece at a time by the blind leading the blind. While Joe was lost in thought, Boris had moved on, leaving a phantom cloud of grey tobacco smoke hanging in the air at face level where he had been standing, before it slowly rose and spread across the ceiling like an expanding, diffuse stain.

The jazz club was filling as the post-dinner and movie crowds arrived in search of booze and swing. Lily had to return to her bar duties. His first thought had been of a tuxedoed magician from some old comic, with a slim moustache and maybe wearing a domino mask, called Mandrake, but then he remembered it was also a plant, rumoured to have an aphrodisiac effect, among other particularities. More of a root than an actual tree. A forest of mandrake trees sounded improbable. He would have to research it online when he was next at his laptop.

He abandoned himself to people watching. A retired writer in search of characters? The music resumed, but Boris and his trumpet were now playing second fiddle to the piano player exercising his be-bop, while his musical partners looked bored or uninterested.

Lily and Joe were, for the time being, staying in a small hotel on the rue Monsieur le Prince, near the Odéon in the Latin Quarter, in a diminutive room on the top floor. They had to hold their breath to fit into the exiguous lift as it made its clunky upwards progress. She appeared happy to be reunited with him, but there was also a distance he felt in their relationship now, both in and out of bed; she adamantly refused to discuss the events in Venice. Was she blaming him for having accidentally discovered the odd bookshop?

Boris had arranged to meet Joe in the lobby the day following their initial encounter; Lily had excused herself. She wanted to visit the museums, Orsay or the Pompidou Centre. It was, after all, her first time in Paris and she wanted to make the most of it; Joe no longer had the patience or the curiosity for museums. In late afternoon, they would reunite in the Luxembourg Gardens before she had to go work. Joe had assured her she need not work now that he was here, that he could afford their stay in Paris, but she insisted it was better for their relationship if she earned some money by her own means.

Boris was on time and sat in the hotel's art deco lobby jotting down lines in a notebook. He greeted Joe with an expansive wave. It was drizzling outside. They walked over to the Café des Editeurs, just a few steps away on the Carrefour de l'Odéon, where Boris was greeted by a couple of black clad waiters with statutory white aprons like a familiar presence. The bar and restaurant's walls were lined with bookshelves, and walking into the ground floor area felt like a trip back in time to more civilised days, that for Joe evoked the likes of Hemingway and Scott Fitzgerald in their slumming Paris heyday.

They ordered espressos.

"I've been looking into this whole mandrake thing," Boris revealed. "It's both exciting and curious, you know…"

"I was going to myself," Joe said. "But Lily was strangely reluctant for me to do so, so I thought I'd wait and hear what you found."

"There was little of interest in the books in my own collection," Boris indicated. "But I have a friend who's fascinated by all matters relating to the occult. He has a wonderful library, so I visited him this morning."

"The occult?" Joe experienced a wave of discomfort at the prospect. Coincidences and mysteries were OK, but the occult was a step further down a road he was reluctant to consider. He had always been a strong sceptic, scornful of new age theories and the nonsense that surrounded the whole territory.

"Did you know that the mandrake's roots can look bizarrely like a human body, and legend holds it that it can even come in male and female form…"

"So do a fair few other roots and vegetables – carrots, turnips and others. It's just a quirk of nature."

"Yes, but carrots are not known for either their aphrodisiac or medicinal qualities, are they?

"And there is more. There is a myth that states that a demon inhabits the root and that whoever is uprooting it with a view to stealing it and taking advantage of its properties will be pursued and killed by the demon. In another volume, I read that when it is uprooted, the mandrake is often heard to scream!"

"Just fanciful stories…"

Boris looked down at his notes and read out a few lines, which he'd copied from an obscure text. "'The humanoid-shaped mandrake root, or *Mandragora officinarum*, was widely believed to be produced by the semen of hanged men under the gallows. Alchemists claimed that hanged men ejaculated after their necks were broken and that the earth absorbed their final 'strengths'. In some versions, it is blood instead of semen. The root itself was often used in ancient times in love philters and potions, while its fruit was said to facilitate pregnancies. Witches who "made love" to the mandrake root were said to produce offspring that had no feelings of real love and had no soul.' Fancy that."

"It does ring a bell, reading about those things ages ago," Joe remarked.

Boris theatrically slammed the pages of his notebook together. "And then I remembered," he said. "Have you heard of *The Manuscript Found in Saragossa*?"

"I'm familiar with it but never read it, Maybe saw a Polish movie adaptation."

"You must read it. A masterpiece, but sadly unfinished despite its various iterations. Initially it's like a more erotic, and violent, version of Boccaccio's *Decameron*, with stories full of strangeness and fury being told to characters who then go on to tell their own stories, and on and on until you get lost in its circles of truth and lies; a veritable hall of mirrors. All a bit of a maelstrom of a plot. Feels so modern even though it was written in the 18th century."

"Who wrote it?" To Joe, it sounded like the sort of book he had always wanted to write but had found himself unable to.

"A Polish aristocrat and politician. Count Jan Potocki."

Joe made a mental note of the name and the book.

"Early on in the novel, it's been years since I read it, I remember a striking scene when it was, I think, the narrator – or at any rate, one of the multiple narrators – who comes across the spectacle of a hanged man on the branch of a deformed tree, and his seed peppering the ground. From which later, mandrakes would come to life."

Joe shuddered. Almost imagining himself with a thick rope around his neck, being hurled into the void, stripped naked, and the impact of the asphyxiation forcing a final erection out of him; death juxtaposed with his last orgasm. He quickly chased the thought away.

He took a hold of himself. "But mandrakes don't grow into trees," he pointed out "They're small, stunted. And if I recall, principally a Mediterranean plant. They would never grow tall enough to create a forest. It's an impossibility."

Boris grinned. "But what a lovely idea it would be, wouldn't it? Rather poetic, eh?"

"You're welcome to it."

"Nah, I have ideas enough for another hundred books and stories. You can have it for free," Boris said. Then sighed. "I have a damaged heart; I will never write those hundred books, I fear."

Mandrake roots. Forests. Impossibilities and improbabilities. But where did the beautiful angels of death – Emma? Lily? – fit into the unholy equation?

The Ways of the Dreamers

They had arranged to have dinner with Boris and his wife Michèle the following week. The couple planned to introduce them to an authentic Moroccan couscous restaurant close to Montparnasse which they assured Lily and Joe was 'the real stuff', unlike so many of the smaller joints dotted around the St Michel area.

However, that same morning Boris died of a heart attack. Joe remembered Boris telling him that his days were numbered, but he didn't realise how close to the truth this had been. Death had been instantaneous, they were assured – a massive stroke; he wouldn't have suffered much pain.

"It's the way he would have wanted it," Joe pointed out. "Me too, when the time comes. I would hate falling to pieces one limb or part failing at a time, each thought crumbling after another, having to endure a living form of death."

Lily gave him a strange look, like a thin cloud travelling across her face, her eyes losing their brilliance, as if reassessing him and her presence at his side. A dawning realisation of the years that stood between them and the incongruity of their relationship. She declared she would not attend Boris' funeral. "I don't like sad occasions," she excused herself. Joe went alone.

The following evening Lily asked him if he could advance her the money to purchase a flight back to Canada. He didn't question her, wanting to part ways with at least a modicum of elegance. He didn't expect to be repaid and readily agreed. "I'm sorry, Joe. So sorry. But the more I think of the days ahead if I stay with you, the more I see matters turning out badly, and there's a voice inside of me whispering that I should not be around when that happens. Maybe it's better for the both of us…" She apologised again and again.

And so she left. For good this time.

There was little to keep him in Paris. He'd only come here because of Lily anyway. He'd lived in the city for many years when he was younger and it was a place so full of bittersweet memories that since his return he had carefully avoided setting foot in certain areas. The Halles, the rue St Denis, Pigalle, Ménilmontant… each held painful shards of a past life strewn with mistakes it was now no longer possible to correct. Of girls, of women, of shattered dreams and inconsolable loneliness. One of his favourite movies, or at any rate one that had left an indelible mark on him, was Louis Malle's *Le Feu Follet*, adapted from the novel by Pierre Drieu la Rochelle. In the film (and the book) a man, having lost his will to live, returns to the Paris of his youthful dreams and dances a waltz between old friends, women he had known, places he had been, silently imploring them all to give him a reason to keep on living, only to be met with a wall of silence or indifference. Finally, surrounded by his memories and his books, he kills himself. A long suicide note, a plea for help. Stark, despairing, in black and white and if he recalled properly even the soundtrack music encouraged you to take a razor blade to your wrists. The actor Maurice Ronet had played the part of the hapless protagonist, heavenly inspired by the author himself, who would take his own life a few years following the book's publication.

Joe had been travelling somewhat aimlessly before Lily. He would just continue. Go where his mood of the day dictated. He no longer had much in the way of ties to a place, a house, reality and he could afford it, so why not. Lily had been a pleasant interlude, even if aspects of his time with her had proven disturbing.

So, where should he go now?

There were interminable plane journeys, with stopovers in liminal and anonymous airports where identical booze and perfumes were sold at duty-free rates regardless of location and tried to make you believe that it mattered not whether you were in Dubai, Shanghai, Abu-Dhabi or Rio de Janeiro, bizarre in-between territories that held little resemblance to the cities that lay beyond the air-conditioned doors of the sprawling harshly-lit airports.

He endured train journeys in bullet trains and rickety, steam-driven convoys of carriages across plains, deserts and mountains and even took some river trips down fabled streams, watching on deck as the boats manoeuvred endless series of locks, their bows scraping dangerously against high concrete walls over which moss grew, green and humid.

Joe no longer counted the days. It all felt immaterial, distant, as if wading his way through a dream of the world. He was neither a tourist nor a mere traveller, more of a flaneur in a universe of dreams, detached, on a road to nowhere that only he could understand as he neglected forking paths or detours and just peered straight ahead, seldom interacting with others and often spending days in which he wouldn't even speak a word to anyone, unless he had to order food or drink or ask for directions. The people he came across on his wanderings were of no interest to him; he was unable to relate to them. Eventually, he had the conviction, he would meet others like himself, dreamers too. And maybe he would finally get some answers. Lily had been one, but he had been unable to hold on to her. The story of his life, but next time, he was determined he would get it right. If there was a next time.

A left turn here, a right turn there. It was a bit like throwing the dice. Which is how he found himself in Exopotamia, and its iteration of New Orleans.

It wasn't even a city, let alone one in Louisiana, bathing in the splendored shadows of swampy bayous or luxuriating in the scent of spices.

Someone had long ago suggested they call the place Samarkand, but it was not situated near a desert, let alone sited in the footsteps of Marco Polo. So the name had not curried favour. But one of the first wave of arrivals to settle here some decades earlier – the precise date was furiously contested – had once visited the real New Orleans and his (or her) taste buds still retained a lingering and affectionate nostalgia for gumbo and oysters on the half shell and he had suggested the name. No one had forcibly objected and the moniker had somehow stuck.

This particular New Orleans was actually set in a plain on a sizeable island in an archipelago at the very centre of the sea of Exopotomia. An island that appeared on few published maps. And which didn't even have a name.

This is where they had all converged. Some had arrived on their own while others had been part of random groups which had then splintered, but they had remained on. They trickled in and never left, as if caught in a spider's cobweb. One dotted with empty skies, personal dreams and memories the exiles kept carefully concealed. It was a bit like the end of the Bangkok hippie trail, but without the dirt or the terrible heat.

A town that did not officially exist, with a borrowed name. But, for now, it was home. Their other New Orleans.

It didn't even have a church. Not that it was a place God had forgotten; more like he had never become aware of its existence.

Nor did it have a jail. Neither God nor law in these heathen parts!

A bunch of them were enjoying coffee at the *Café des Philosophes* one evening. Sharing silences, aimless conversation and killing time.

It was Vernon who brought the subject up.

"Does anyone know who was the first to arrive here and stick around?" he asked.

"Some old timer once told me it was actually Melody..." Sullivan responded.

They all sighed in unison.

Everyone of course knew of Melody, but none had actually met her. It was long before their time. A whole generation or so of travellers ago. It was rumoured she was the first owner of the Hotel Marseilles, where most of them now stayed. Some preferred the river boats, or the caravans, most of which no longer even had wheels, but the Hotel Marseilles had hot water which the sturdy embarkations moored by the nearby lake with no name hadn't.

By all accounts, Melody Nelson had been an incomparable beauty. She hailed from Nova Scotia, had fled an abusive relationship and settled here to hide from either bad men or foreign authorities. She had acquired a plot of land and had the two-storey hotel built by local labourers.

"Was it her decision to call this place New Orleans?" Marie, the Lithuanian pianist who never smiled, asked.

No one knew the answer.

A portrait of Melody still hung behind the hotel bar. She wore a green silk jacket with ornamental buttons which looked vaguely Chinese in style, its collar surrounding her neck like a noose. Her blonde hair flowed down to her shoulders and her eyes were violet. There was a hint of a smile on her lips, almost mischievous, knowing, drawing you into some form of complicity, like a modern Mona Lisa.

They all knew the story well: Melody's first customer at the hotel had been a French jazz trumpet player and they had fallen passionately in love. But the trumpet player had a hole in his heart and the couple were forlornly aware from the very beginning they had no long-term future. He barely lasted past their first summer together before he collapsed while improvising on Gershwin's 'Rhapsody in Blue' on the hotel's forecourt, just a stone's throw from the nearby river Mersey. Melody had been heartbroken. Two years later, she had picked a bunch of black flowers that bloomed by the shore and that all knew to avoid. She ate them and succumbed to their poison within a week, in terrible agony. She left a child, Fleur, from their liaison, who was the present owner of the Hotel Marseilles. Joe had smiled when he had been told the story for the first time; how Boris would have enjoyed the tale.

Another of the itinerant musicians who had travelled to New Orleans alongside the man with the hole in his heart had written a song, which he'd performed at her funeral: 'The Ballad of Melody Nelson'. But it was now considered in bad taste to ever play it on the bar's juke box.

"I heard say that while they were still together, Melody and the trumpet player with a hole in his heart managed to fuck in every single room of the hotel…" Prince Rupert said. He was allegedly from minor European royalty and had fled his family home in disgrace, landing there many years later. He considered himself something of a lady's man, although none of them were aware of any single woman in their group of misfits and refugees from reality having actually been bedded by him, let alone feeling an iota of attraction to his unctuous manners and persona.

"Next you'll be telling us their rutting ghosts still haunt the hotel rooms…" someone remarked, debunking him.

Night was falling as most of the customary crowd Joe had fallen in with departed the café in single file. To their respective hotel rooms, their rental apartments or the fleet of houseboats on the river. The sun was fading across the faraway mountains of the sea, that shimmering, liminal zone where the water faded into the line of the horizon and merged with infinity. It was autumn, but in their hearts most of the old crowd still wanted it to be spring.

He watched as Lora walked hand in hand with Tristan to whichever sofa they were squatting on tonight. Joe sighed. Just another manic pixie beauty of the type he felt instantly attracted to, defying all logic. They had barely exchanged more than a few words since he had arrived in Exopotomia. He had briefly thought he had a remote chance of 'clicking' with her; that she might become his much sought after final passion. Something about the way she spoke to him and moved. But, again, a curse that now followed him wherever he went, she was too young and he was too old, and who can win when the other guy in the imaginary triangle also happened to be a poet. At any rate, Joe had resolved to write a story about her soon. It would be his last tale. It would be word perfect. That would be the way to go. Prose survived and poetry died, transient as it was. The literary odds were weighted in his favour, even if the real-life ones had him pegged as a non-starter. Joe already had the first paragraph in draft form and was determined to begin writing the imaginary tale in earnest the following day.

The only problem was that he had absolutely no clue as to what he should be writing about. Yes Lora, or a young woman resembling her in every detail, would certainly feature. It would be a love story with bizarre characters. But beyond that, he was totally at sea. In truth, he had little left to say, had run out of stories to tell. Running on fumes, vague shards of his past tales full of sound, fury and downbeat endings. Maybe he should have accepted the evidence that his writing career had come to an end. All his stories told and the world remained the same: he knew he had made no noticeable difference. He had given much thought to all those titles he had caught an all-too-brief sight of on that bookshelf at *Il Sogno*, in Venice, and come to realise they were all ideas he had once considered but had never written about. A library of the damned, of imaginary books that the world was better without. Maybe, during the course of their many pillow conversations, he had mentioned one of those nebulous ideas to Lily and seeing it come somehow alive had spooked her right from the outset. Although she had suggested she had seen herself on the actual page. All confusing in retrospect.

Little did Joe know that the movie makers would be arriving in town. And that his surreal ballet of stuttering relationships would be shattered once and for all.

They were some thousand miles East of nowhere and never more than three hours from the sea.

The ramshackle town had begun with a gas station, which soon went out of business as there were no roads nearby. Just dirt tracks leading in and out of a narrow plain through which the river flowed. No cars.

The pumps remained, rusting, like minute Stonehenge or Easter Island figures. Marking their equator, the centre of a forlorn circle of abandonment. Later someone raised some shacks built of wooden planks and with coruscated metal roofs to keep the elements at bay. It seldom rained around here, but the winds followed seasonal patterns and sometimes raged. Albeit always at night, as if cannily aware they were keeping the settlers awake throughout.

There was talk on the island of a possible railway line that would be built, bisecting it, and the rumour attracted further folk and the town grew in small increments. Dreamers, rapscallions, cloud poets, would be captains of enterprise, fugitives, singers hoping to craft the perfect song, tattoo artists and scoundrels. You could always count on artists to make up the numbers. Some pretended to be composers of unwritten symphonies, others were dancers about architecture; a tribe of fools and their entourage, men and women who held on with ferocity to their original sense of innocence like babies refusing to relinquish their rubber dummies as they grew older and heavier, sycophants and soldiers of fortune seeking out a new, improbable war. A man like Joe, who now mostly wrote books in his head, easily fitted the bill.

He came much later and inadvertently became a repository for the tales, the lies and the stories about the growth of the other New Orleans. Of how, building by building, it began to spread, branching out in a circular motion away from its heart, the Hotel Marseilles, and backing up to it the obligatory bank, Baxter and Sons, which also doubled up as a post office.

An unreliable old timer had related the story of how Melody Nelson's father had arrived a couple of generations back, with his child bride in tow and, allegedly, sacks of gold, after eloping with not just her but her valuable dowry, only to see his wife succumb in childbirth.

And then there was the Butterfly Kid, who hailed from San Francisco, whose real name was Chester so who could blame him for adopting a different sobriquet? He opened the Stone Museum, consisting principally of displays of amber he had accumulated on his travels, and later helped build the theatre where all the town artists performed once they had been vetted by the Council of Contrarian Philosophers, a group of freaks who steadfastly refused to set foot in the *Café des Philosophes* because of a long-standing rift between their respective creeds, Sartre vs. Nietzsche or Lacan vs. Husserl, or something like that. When they drank too much, which was often the case, they would come to blows, settling their differences in the wounding fields by the creek, in the south-eastern fields on the edge of the ever-growing town.

And then there was the Fellowship of Angels. All women who had travelled here from the four corners of the globe and self-appointed themselves as guardians of the forest which lay close to the river, whose calm waters fed its sprawling roots. There was talk of it being haunted, of the screams of men wafting through its branches in the dead of night, but the place was so full of tall stories that no one took this one particularly seriously.

It must have felt like being on the set of a spaghetti western, contradictory buildings rising almost overnight, seemingly in geometrical opposition to each other, crazy patterns outlined against the night sky, battling shapes and materials, a gentle form of anarchy, of madness, that was more quaint than dangerous. The only thing the ersatz New Orleans lacked was a town sheriff, a hangman or domestic animals roaming the dusty streets to conform with Sergio Leone western standards.

And, by default, Joe became its involuntary chronicler. What else can a writer do when his job is done and he has run out of his own narratives?

Somehow word of the haphazard enclave leaked and reached the outside world, and soon arrivals doubled – further dreamers, more lost souls. And someone had the bright idea of setting a movie here. The railway never came, but the mirages of the silver screen did.

Their metal silver trailers, their money, the giant generators, the cranes, the carpenters and electricians, the handymen, the gofers, the hangers-on and the grips. The suits amongst them marvelled at the environment, the creatives gazed in amazement, but following an initial wave of enthusiasm their moods darkened when they realised the script they had brought with them could not be filmed here. Some major mistake at the production head office.

The actual producers who flew in weekly by helicopter had acquired the movie rights to an obscure French novel with a surrealist bent, entitled *The Red Grass*, but the director who had brought them the project soon came to realise that *A*, the script some Hollywood hack had come up with was unfilmable here; *B*, it made no sense either; and *C*, they would not be allowed to dye the limited patches of grass that circled the town red, or any other colour for that matter.

Eventually, the executives and the visiting big name stars left, but much of the minor 'talent' remained, charmed by the lazy rhythms of the laid-back lifestyle here. Or all too aware that life on the outside presented no improvement.

Within a month or so of the film being abandoned, New Orleans reverted back to its routine, albeit with its population double the size, its tribes strengthened in numbers. Joe now felt like an old-timer here but still thought himself a stranger in a strange land, akin to a wanderer who had been summoned here with no idea of his purpose, but knowing the answers were just an inch away, tantalising him, scaring him.

And why, oh why, were so many of the women here so fucking beautiful? It just defied the law of averages.

The Ways of Stories

Alraune had never liked the name she was given by her progenitor, and often told people she had once been called Claudia. She was German and born in Hannover. She always wore black and had a tattoo of a tree branch running down from her shoulders to her sublimely rounded arse cheeks. Or maybe it was a weeping willow? Joe had never had the opportunity of viewing its roots in her holy of holies. She had come to New Orleans to work make-up on the movie that was never made, but had also been promised a small walk-on part by one of the executive producers who wanted to get inside her pants. He didn't. But that did not deter the single men around who persisted in that worthy ambition. She was also a member of the Fellowship of Angels, marked as such by a distinctive tattoo outlining a mandrake root on her wrist, but this was a subject she would never discuss with men should it be raised in a conversation. Those were the rules of the group.

Alraune stayed on when the movie bunch retreated to more propitious terrain and subject. This was as good a place as any to live, she reckoned.

She now worked behind the counter at the café.

She had come off shift. It was night, the fragrances of the island drifted by, carried by a soft semi-tropical breeze; bougainvillea, exotic smells of cooking from the campsites crisscrossing the town, a delicate cocktail that caressed the senses, and one of the reasons Joe had some years back opted to remain here and travel no further, so unlike the scent of big cities full of decay, stale beer and silent despair.

Alraune was distant tonight. Joe, a familiar sight at the café, did not dare ask her why, afraid she might tell him she missed her old life and might be contemplating a return to the mainland.

He raised his glass to her.

"Long day?"

"I guess so. Sometimes I get tired having to stay so polite to customers and forcing myself to be cheerful throughout," she said.

"I wouldn't want to work as a waitress, let alone a waiter…"

Her skin was porcelain white, her cheeks flushed, the black of her work outfit clinging to her skin, highlighting its pallor. She had green eyes. The patterns of her visible tattoos flowed like small rivers across the length of her body.

"Sad?" he asked her.

"More like dreamy, you know. Feeling a bit lost. Not sure I can explain it properly."

"The blues?"

"Maybe. Why do they call it that? That particular colour? Should be more like the greys, no?"

"I'd never thought of it that way…"

"What about you, Mister Storyteller, what makes you remain here. Unless I'm mistaken, you're not particularly happy either?"

"Ah, the million-dollar question!"

"I can't quite afford that much," she remarked. She dug into her pocket and pulled out a coin and offered it to Joe. "I'm a cheapskate sort of girl. Will that pay for a story?"

"Now we're talking. A man can't live on royalties alone..."

"Deal!"

"So what sort of story appeals to you today, Miss Alraune, named after a minor demon?"

"A sad one, naturally"

"Those are the only ones I know."

"How did I ever guess?"

"Any plans for the night?" Joe enquired. "Can I be your Scheherazade and serenade you with stories until dawn breaks." He pocketed the coin she had proffered.

"And if your tales displease me, might I have your head chopped off when morning comes, if I remember the legend correctly? Or any such more modern variation?"

"A risk well worth taking..."

At worst, if he ran out of stories to serenade Alraune's angst, he could always rely on ChatGPT to galvanise his failing imagination.

But would he ever last a thousand and one nights?

They settled on seven nights only. If he could make her cry she would come to his bed. Should he fail, it was metaphorically off with his head; Joe was uncertain how serious she was, but nothing ventured, nothing gained – or lost – he guessed.

There was the story of Colin and Chloé. Colin had fallen for her in a big way. But Chloé had a venomous flower blooming inside her lungs and no medicine known to man could nip it in the bud before it grew even more deadly and killed her. Colin hoped against hope but Chloé knew all too well what had given birth to the flower that was eating her up from inside: it was the ghosts of all the other men she had foolishly gifted herself to before, each of which had stolen a further inch of her soul and left a barren patch in their wake. Users who had not even loved her truly, but had taken advantage of her, plundered her body, enjoyed the pleasure of penetrating her without imparting even an ounce of joy. Their presence lingered, malevolent, spreading, like a shadow against the sun of her heart and no medicine man the couple consulted in their desperation could find a solution, an antidote. Tears had no effect. So, they partied extravagantly with their friends, a collection of endearing eccentrics, until time ran out. There was only one way the story could end. With grief.

"I've actually read that book and seen the movie,' Alraune declared, "but your version is too nihilistic." She took a kitchen knife from the nearby counter and gently pressed it against his throat. "Try again."

In a city called New Orleans, which bore little resemblance to theirs and luxuriated by the shores of the mighty Mississippi river, a young Italian woman called Giulia was fleeing her demons and was followed there by her older lover, while the rest of the country was overtaken by a bitter civil war, and the state of Louisiana (as well as California, Maine and a few others) declared independence and seceded from the rest of the United States. However, by the time he reached the city following picaresque adventures on the river, she had now become the captive of a local magician and had her memory erased and no longer recognised him. In a bid to save her, the older man volunteered to relinquish his own memories in the hope they could meet again as new people altogether and somehow rekindle the flame that had once burned so strong. But by then, the new Giulia had married a local journalist, closer in age to her, and blanked him when he engineered a meeting, as if he were a total stranger.

"Do I note some autobiographical elements and, in your apocalyptic tale, does Louisiana become a Republic?" Alraune asked, the sharp end of her knife caressing the wafer-thin skin of his neck. "Try again."

Joe briefly wondered what it would feel like to be decapitated. How long his consciousness would survive, thoughts, pain, white lights and all?

On the third night Alraune was not wearing waitress black, but a short white linen dress that didn't reach further than her mid-thigh, offering a tantalising glimpse of the multi-coloured ink and foliage running down her right leg, raising terrible lust in his heart as to where it took root above, between her legs.

Joe told her the story of the trumpet player of St Germain des Prés.

He was a man with too many talents. As a result, people wouldn't take him seriously. Just an entertainer, a dilettante, they said. He was a gifted musician, whose love of traditional jazz ran deep through his veins. He dreamed endlessly of travelling to New Orleans, the city on the Mississippi, the birthplace of jazz in Basin Street, that mythical street where Louis Armstrong, Sidney Bechet and so many others had practiced their early craft, and he sat in awe at the feet of the

American musicians who had serenaded him and a whole generation of post-war French intellectuals in the smoky cellars and crowded clubs of St Germain des Prés. But he also wrote. Novels that didn't fit anywhere and didn't conform to the parameters of his acquaintances Albert Camus and Jean-Paul Sartre in the heyday of existentialism; his books were just not serious enough, bizarre, unrealistic; he translated pulp American novels, hardboiled stuff and science fiction; wrote avant-garde plays and song lyrics. He even adopted a pseudonym to pen a schlocky thriller in the American-style which everyone assumed was the real thing and managed to attract the attention of the censors and outsold all his other books, those that came from the heart. How ironic for a man whose heart suffered from an irregular beat. And still he had ideas for more. When his pulp novel sold to the movies, he knew they would fail to understand its innate sense of irony and would just come up with a literal, vulgar adaptation. Which they did. And he died of a heart attack one morning in a screening room on the Champs Elysées in Paris, just as the producers were about to screen a preview copy of the movie for him. He was still much too young.

Alraune remarked "Isn't it always the case that genius is seldom recognised in its lifetime?"

Joe nodded.

She was a hard nut to crack. With not an inch of sentimentality to spare. But then what should he have expected from a woman whose name in legend originated from the sinister tale of a prostitute impregnated, in a laboratory by a mad professor, with the semen of a hanged murderer and cursed thereafter to have no soul or ability to love?

But the pressure of the kitchen knife she had been moving from hand to hand while he recited his story lessened against his carotid artery. She wouldn't cut him tonight, he realised. Was that an elusive sentiment of disappointment cruising around his mind?

On the fourth night, Joe elected to tell her a story full of magic and colour. It was the tale of a mysterious costumed ball that had been going on for a few centuries, migrating yearly, and that had become the stuff of legend. Ball? Orgy? Ritual? Tales would fly from ear to ear, speculation brewed, but only past participants knew the truth about it and they were sworn to secrecy. All that was known was the fact the ball had a Queen, the Mistress of Night and Dawn, and every generation a new Queen was crowned in a public ceremony that was shocking and beautiful to behold, and that even millionaires and true royalty would not dare to repeat its savage splendour. She was selected when still a child by the courtiers of the ball, who carried the flame and dictated the rules which remained unchanged through the passing of the centuries. Always an orphan, her life was closely monitored until she became of age. Until the night of the ball, she would remain a virgin, although her education had carefully emphasised that the pleasure of the senses was the most wonderful of life's attainments and it was seen that the future Queen would, until the day came, be kept on terrible edge, her body aflame with lust and desire, craving for the little death of consummation. Then, as the night of the ball finally arrived, she would be led naked to the altar around which the festivities were about to be triggered, laid out, washed, placed on satin sheets and tied into position. Then, at the stroke of midnight, when the music began, every man present, each a suitor carefully selected both for his amorous skills and his girth, would approach her crucified body and gently mount her. But through the miracle of the ball, on every occasion the future Queen would orgasm, a tattoo would appear on her body, risen from unknown depths, and flower across the unbelievable pallor of her skin, in a furious frenzy of wild colours, patterns, images and the most exquisite of calligraphies. First a teardrop, below her left eye. Then, as she came for the second time, a scarlet rose above her heart. Men would breed her in quick succession, with a soft soliloquy of love reaching her ears while they thrust inside her. Wonderfully obscene words in a parade of languages dotting her body, a wide-open eye between her navel and her bruised cunt; a painted heart surrounding her spread labia; a spider's web circling her nipples; a dagger along her side; on and on the images appeared as she sighed, writhed, cried tears of joy, wet herself, invoked God as a concentric wave of abominable pleasure raced outwards from her genitalia and rushed like electricity through her body, every limb and extremity on fire, her mind ablaze as she gradually assumed her royalty. Until, at dawn, every man spent, her bindings were severed and she rose to her feet to stand in her terrible nudity, her people below her, with not an inch of her body unillustrated, unpainted, with the exception of her face, still flushed with every emotion she had travelled through between night and dawn, where the legacy of her very first orgasm, the delicate, miniscule tear-drop, was the only tattoo to be seen. And then the Queen smiled and greeted her people...

"You sure have a talent for dirty stories,' Alraune remarked. Joe blushed. "That was wild... But a bit unrealistic, hey? No woman could... hmm... entertain... that many men without a serious risk to her health, not to mention delicate parts of her anatomy, no?"

"God only knows what it says about me... That I'm just a dirty old man?"

"Can I be the judge of that?"

She had left the knife on the table throughout. An enigmatic smile passed across her full lips.

"Your stories might save you," Alraune whispered conspiratorially. "But then again they may not..." She paused, staring at Joe intently. "Can I be deadly serious?"

"Of course."

A tremor of excitement ran through his body. He was tired, but apprehensive, strangely aware he had reached an important fork in the road and that revelations were imminent. The air was still.

"Will you accept your fate if you fail the seven days test?"

Despite the pressure of the knife, he had never believed she would slit his throat. It would prove too messy.

"You're right. It is much too messy. All that blood and such." As if she was reading his mind.

"I would," he finally agreed.

"I promise it will be painless."

Like a pact. Joe nodded.

"Good," Alraune said. They had reached a crucial juncture. Had it been a movie, the musical soundtrack would have reached its crescendo right now.

"You can tell me your next story tomorrow night, Joseph Modiano. But first let me treat you with a tale of my own."

Joe nodded.

"A long time ago, I almost died. I had become a stupid junkie, heavily into drugs and suffered an overdose. It was in Rio de Janeiro at Carnival time. Crazy days. I'd fallen in with bad people. I was inches away from the point of no return. In my enfeebled condition, a quarter here and three quarters floating away into eternal sleep, I thought I could even see that fabled white light calling for me. But I was saved. A whore from the favelas took pity on me, and… I will spare you the unsavoury details… forcibly fed me the seed of a dying man who had also overdosed alongside me, victim of the same poisonous stuff. And, when I came to, she called me Alraune. It was only later that I found out why. But there was a price to pay. By involuntarily accepting the seed that saved me, I had de facto been enrolled into the Fellowship of Angels. As she had been herself and many generations of women before us…"

Joe felt a chill wind caressing his cheeks; goose pimples erupted across his exposed limbs. Putting one and one together.

"Your role is to hunt, extract the seed of men?"

"Yes, but they must be dying men. That's where the magic and the horror entwine.

"And must the men be willing?"

"Preferably. It makes their seed more potent."

"And what happens to the seed you have harvested?"

"That's for us to know, Joe."

"And how do you find your sacrificial men?"

"When you become an angel, you learn how to read them, you get a feel for the state of their soul, you quickly come to recognise those who are ready. We are in no rush. We're not like whores of death skulking around dark alleys seeking bodies, men knifed in fights or with needles in their arms. We have a type. You'd be surprised how many actually welcome a release from this life of sorrows we all travel through…"

Yes, Joe knew.

The Ways of Lives Past

Night five. A delicate breeze blew through the café's terrace. Alraune was wearing black again, and in the growing penumbra Joe could see how the light of the full moon shone strong, spreading like quicksilver across her bare forearms.

"So what does my dirty old man have in store for me tonight?" asked Alraune the angel.

It was the story of a man who felt he no longer had valid reasons to live. He was tortured by grief, loneliness and guilt for all the times he had done the wrong thing. His home was a repository of memories, things, object, clothes, thousands of books, photos, much amber jewellery, all the detritus that the years accumulate. So, he travelled. For a short while, the lure of exotic places partly filled the void inside him but he quickly ran out places to visit, to roam. Once you've seen the walls of one old city or two, observed the sun set in the tropics like an orb of fire crowning the line of the horizon, night after sultry night, you feel you've seen them all. Quickly, cities, beaches, islands all merged in his mind and brought him no joy. He had read too many novels full of crass romanticism in which the main characters travelled in search of truth, experience or salvation. He had actually attempted to write one himself. He was on the balcony of a cheap hotel in a city in the southern hemisphere watching the waves, and the surfers cascading between them, as the early morning distant, cold sun attempted to break the barricades of the clouds, when at the opposite end of the beach he spotted a curious shape sprawled across the sand. It looked like a mermaid. He cleaned his glasses and looked again. It was most definitely a real-life mermaid. She sat there, forlorn, her head bowed, water lapping against her outstretched body. No one else appeared to have noticed her. He walked down to the beach and approached her. She looked up at him; her hair was tangled with thin strands of seaweed and her tail shimmered like a wake of diamonds. He couldn't help but stare at her breasts; they were just perfect. Firm, small, dark-nippled, like ripe fruit begging to be harvested. She was called Megan. She had cheekbones to die for. Over the following fortnight, he fell in love with her. He knew it made no sense, but as the cliché goes, the heart has its reasons. They found an isolated cove where they could not be disturbed. She allowed him to touch her, they kissed and as he expected she tasted of salt water. He brushed her hair with all the delicacy he could summon; she took his manhood in her mouth and remarked his emissions reminded her of oysters. But there were limits to their lust, the obstacle of contrasting anatomies. She sulked. He hurt inside. Then one day, as they lay in the sand, listening to their respective heartbeats, she told him there was a way. But he would have to sacrifice his penis in the process. He knew better than to ask further questions or query the details. Arrangements were made; Megan knew of a willing surgeon in the nearest coastal town who could operate on him. Then, she revealed, once the procedure had been completed, he would be in a position to follow her beneath the sea. He agreed. The doctor castrated him. It was agreed that it would take a fortnight or so for him to heal properly and then he and Megan could meet again and be together. The endless hours went by all so slowly. But the day came. Early dawn, he descended to the beach in their isolated cove, shed his clothes and stood there naked, emasculated, uneasy. In the distance, he could see Megan the mermaid waiting. She was more beautiful than ever. She was smiling. Or was it more of a satisfied leer? He stepped closer to her. And saw she was now wearing a heavy necklace. He neared. And his heart missed a beat when he had full sight of the necklace. Around a rough piece of rope hung a dozen or so men's cocks in all shapes and length. His eyes were drawn to his own, fixed to the string holding them by a hook through his ball sack. He was frozen to the spot as Megan retreated and disappeared through the rising waves without as much as a farewell. The mermaid from the southern seas had completed her necklace.

"Wow," Alraune the angel of death exclaimed. "That's truly wicked."

"You liked the tale?"

"Absolutely... I just hope it's not autobiographical or wishful thinking..."

Joe lowered his eyes.

On what would turn out to be their final night of storytelling, Alraune invited her purveyor of sad stories to the caravan which she rented, parked in the café's car park. She normally shared it with another waitress from the café, but her friend was absent tonight. She allowed him to chastely sleep beside her until dawn broke across the simmering sealine.

"I had an affair with a married woman called Kate. I was also married at the time. I'd come across her at a conference and had immediately fallen in lust with her and brazenly written her a letter declaring the fact. We worked in the same industry. In nine cases out of ten, this sort of approach never works, but there must have been a confluence of moons and moods and she did not answer negatively. We met up for a drink, in a pub by Cambridge Circus, skirted the subject endlessly but it was immediately apparent that she was not immune to me, and was unsettled in her marriage, and my indecent proposal out of the blue had her similarly not so much lusting after me, but craving for something different in her life. As I drove her to her railway station following our first meeting, she took hold of my hand and, in a low voice, just said 'Yes, I will.' I was overjoyed. We booked a hotel room by Heathrow airport, and I brought along a bottle of white wine and a punnet of strawberries. The affair began. My office after hours, rutting over the carpet in the staff room; holding hands at bad movies in darkened cinemas where no one knew us; at another conference in Brighton where we only left the room to eat and spent all our time fucking with the energy of despair. The sex was good, as to be expected from sensualists who had respectively been in long marital relationships that had inevitably become a tad stale. One evening as I was inside her, she asked me to hold her hands down harder, to be rougher with her. It went against my natural instinct but I did, enjoying the rapture it brought to her face, her lips trembling, her whole body responding in turn, her wild Medusa-like hair a labyrinth of curls in disarray. Another time, she asked me to choke her gently. It escalated quickly, until the day we were faced with choices about the way ahead. I was willing to jettison my marriage, my children. Kate hesitated. We were apart for the duration of a long business trip to Omaha in Nebraska, a place I found out to be the dark hole of nowhere. By the time I returned, Kate had opted to remain with her husband, and called a halt to our relationship. I screamed her name silently in my sleep; I raged against my fate; I wrote terrible pornographic stories in which her avatar suffered the worst of indignities. But life went on. I began reflecting on our time together, how she submitted to me in such intimate ways beyond the vanilla sex we had both previously been accustomed to. I began to speculate about the nature of sexual submission, how one person could offer themselves so completely to another, with no limits, no shame, no sense of decency. I had always been a particularly sexual person and the memory of Kate and her hidden nature was like an itch I couldn't scratch. I sought out other women, other affairs, but none could match the beauty of Kate and the gift she could orchestrate of her body and mind. One twisted thought led to another. I had often speculated what it felt like for a woman to take a man's cock into her mouth and suck it. An itch, I knew. One day, I succumbed to a Craigslist ad and met another man, got down on my knees and opened my mouth. I had never been attracted to other men in the slightest, but I found out, to my surprise and shame, that I was attracted to their penises, had an out of body experience watching myself sucking anonymous cocks, belonging to men whose faces I would never even care to remember. It was a kind of submission. In my folly, I identified with Kate and all the other women who had once fellated me. One thing would lead to another and soon I submitted fully to strangers. Was taken anally by them, mounted in the same sexual position Kate had always preferred. I hadn't become gay, but somehow feeling myself being filled to the hilt, past the initial pain due to my tightness, I began to understand the women I had known, those with whom I had enjoyed sex. My own sexual history had begun, years ago, in France, where I lived and feasted on the books of Boris Vian, André Pieyre de Mandiargues, Pierre Drieu la Rochelle and Aragon; all men who loved women intensely. I justified my increasing number of anonymous sexual encounters with strange men – very seldom was I used by the same one more than twice – by the fact that I could now understand how women felt and therefore begin to know the unknowable minds of women, and now felt so much closer to them by virtue of being used as they were, and frequently so. The internet is a great enabler and I had great success in advertising myself as a mature submissive and making myself available for free to all-comers. Both pimp and whore. On the FetLife website, a social network for active BDSM practitioners, I perved on others with the same cravings, on both sides of the sexual divide and also that ravine that stood between, full of every kink under the sun. Of late, I had been following a sub in Antarctica who called herself Maoripoet, and had developed a strong attraction to her. Touched myself to photos of her in lingerie, naked, genitalia and openings, on occasion, in the process of being used by men only the sex of which could be seen penetrating her. She posted regular poems, naïve but touching, almost like haikus of lust and cravings, sometimes misspelled, but my heart opened up to her and her quiet radiance; I read her wish list of advertised kinks which she was slowly ticking off: being fucked inside a car, in the rain, at a party, as part of a threesome, roughly, and all the things she still aspired too: a delightful catalogue of sex, excess and deviance I could easily compare to my own in my submissive role. Bizarre thoughts of contacting her and making an indecent offer to join her as part of a couple and enjoy our submissive status together and enjoy the same users, cocks, and rude attentions. But she lived half a world away, was less than half my age. My sister soul in submission. Beauteous curves, red hair, a slightly boy-ish face with a definite touch of humour in the curl of her lips, almost demure in appearance, her repository of cravings concealed from the outside world. So, one day, I wrote a story for her in hope of reaching out in some unconventional sort of way, on the assumption that poets and writers went well together. I sent it as a lengthy message through the website. She blocked me and I lost all possible contact with her!"

"Oh, that is SO sad," Alraune said. "I can't think of anything sadder," she added.

"Neither can I," Joe confessed. How could he not?

And then Alraune finally took him to her bed.

The Ways of Sacrifice

Discretion is the better part of valour. But Alraune was the first bona fide angel he had mated with, and no doubt the last. He knew his performance that short night was poor; he had difficulty even achieving an erection, but he could now die happy knowing that Alraune, of the Fellowship of Angels, had momentarily been his. He'd fucked an angel! And, in the process, had inevitably fallen in love with her enigmatic smile and the twinkle in her eye when she muttered "I want you inside me" and opened her legs wide to him. Although he half reckoned it was also an act of charity. Or a bribe to lead him willingly to what would come next.

In a more traditional story, maybe Joe would now learn to play the trumpet and let his sounds unfurl like clouds over New Orleans, surrounded by the lapping waves of the sea of Exopotamia, and live with an angel until the end of eternity. Or, alternately, he could go travelling again and visit Peking in the autumn? No, not Beijing as it is now known, but rather the Peking that never was.

However, he had expressed his assent to the angel and still thought of himself as a good person, one who stood by his word.

Yes, it was time. He would have no regrets. He would go through with it.

He had travelled the world widely. He had sailed down the Yangtze River and passed through the Three Gorges; he had savoured the roast duck at the Water Margin in London's Golders Green and the Lamb Tikka at the Ganges on Gerrard Street, the oysters at the Acme Oyster House on Iberville Street and the braised beef tongue at Dostoyevsky's in Cologne; he'd visited 35 countries, not counting islands; he had lived in Paris in the spring when young women roamed the streets with the innocence of youth, almost asking to be swept off their feet and elegantly seduced; he had spent time in Italy in the winter when the fog came down from the mountains to smother the plain; he'd spent days at sea watching the calming swirl of the waters and the hypnotic swells punctuating its surface and felt humbled in the extreme; he'd seen movies and read books that had made him cry; he had walked over frozen lava streams and flown above the Sahara desert and some of Africa's jungles; he had known the joy of women, the six he had loved and the several handfuls who had sex with him; he'd had children and grandchildren and marvelled at the miracle of life as they each in turn took their first faltering steps; he'd been to the Mediterranean, the Maldives, Sri Lanka, the Yucatan, Hong Kong, Panama City and the Greek Islands and sprawled naked on some of those faraway exotic beaches when the law allowed; he'd witnessed with his own eyes the sheer, ineffable beauty of well over a hundred cunts and each one had been unique and a sight to behold and never forget; what now felt like years ago, he had even written some books that a few people actually read, although Lily the Newfoundland waitress was the only genuine reader he had met, and the editor who'd acquired his final novel had confessed its ending had made her cry, which Joe was unsure was a good thing or not. He'd lived. Although he had always felt that maybe there was more to life than living. Without a doubt, a glass half-empty sort of man.

"It will be quite painless." Alraune advised him. "I give you my promise."

"And what will happen to my body afterwards?" Joe asked.

"We will lay you to rest by the forest and, one day, if you have been fertile, a tree will bear your name."

The night before his death, Joe had a terrible nightmare in which his feverish imagination recalled a scene from Octave Mirbeau's *The Torture Garden*. In his mind, it was set in China, in ancient times. A man was tied to a wooden post, stripped from the waist downwards and his genitalia exposed. A long queue of 'executioners' would face him, take hold of his penis and vigorously masturbate him in turn, while he remained unsure if they were men or women. Even as the victim fought the pleasure rising inside his bowels, he couldn't avoid orgasming, watching his ejaculate spring from his captive cock and fall to the ground. But that was only the beginning. Joe guessed he had been given some special potion to retain his hardness throughout and as soon as he had come the first time, a new 'executioner' would take a firm hold of his still quivering sex and masturbate him again until he orgasmed a second time, this time with less of an emission. And then a third, and a fourth, and so on. Each new orgasm would come with a scream emanating in his gut as the torture grew ever more powerful, turning what had once been pleasure into an excruciating form of pain, like a sharp knife being twisted around his innards and stabbing the sheer fabric of his brain. Soon his cock had no more ejaculate to express and the successive orgasms only drew blood from his urethra, first drops, then the volume swelling to an abominable flow. Eventually, broken both physically and mentally, literally exsanguinated through his penis, the man died, his mind turned to mulch, his tortured member dripping final red drops like a leaking tap to the bloody ground.

No, Joe remembered, Alraune had assured him the process would be painless.

He trusted her.

Who can you trust, if not an angel?

It was the magic hour, those fleeting minutes before sunset when daylight is redder and softer than when the sun is higher in the sky.

Joe had an inkling of what was about to happen but tried not to dwell on it. He hadn't slept well, but then he had not expected to.

Alraune crept around the bedroom to avoid disturbing him, but he was no longer sleeping. She brought him a glass of grapefruit juice once she noticed his eyes were open and kissed his forehead with a tenderness that had no equal; affectionate, full of sorrow, grateful, melancholy, a farrago of feelings translated into the furtive touch of moist lip against dry skin.

He drank. Savouring the bitterness of the juice and how its underlay of sweetness rushed from his taste buds to his throat and then settled down in the pit of his stomach, quenching his thirst.

"Close your eyes," Alraune asked him.

He did.

Then, cushioned in the newly-formed darkness, he heard the pitter-patter of feet, others entering the room but respecting the silence as if they were in a church, the swirls of air being gently displaced by the movement of unknown bodies as they approached the bed where he lay. Then, another kiss grazing his forehead and a woman's voice just saying his name, 'Joe', and the musky smell of her nearby skin lapping across his senses. He held his breath. His heart beat the light fantastic. A new silence that lasted an eternity and another furtive movement as yet another person leaned over to kiss him. 'Joe' she also said. Her breath smelled of almonds. He realised he was now at the centre of a beautiful ritual and every angel in New Orleans was queuing up to give him his semblance of final rites. He never knew there were so many angels here, and he had now lived in the place for over a year. Or was every female inhabitant of this remote part of Exopotamia an actual angel? Hidden from reality, lurking, patiently waiting for the next sacrificial man to appear and willingly accept his chosen fate. Their very own Wicker Man.

One's breath smelled of roses, another of the sea, and yet another was draped in the fragrance of some exotic, green-tinged exotic perfume. That could only have been Lora. And then there was the one who approached not just in silence but without even disturbing the air that floated between them, like a ghost, immaterial, her kiss emerging out of nowhere when he was least expecting it. He was convinced it was Emma but overcame the temptation to open his eyes and check.

Joe stopped counting.

He was overcome by the abominable tenderness of the occasion. This reverent blessing like no other.

The ceremony of the kisses couldn't have lasted more than ten minutes at most, but time had stretched to infinity and Joe felt a wonderful sense of calm and resignation. One final kiss, warm breath undulating in front of his eyes, and he awaited the next one. But it didn't come. The first part of the ritual was over.

"You may open your eyes," Alraune said. Joe was expecting a battalion of angels to be standing around the bed, watching him, observing him, but Alraune was now alone with him. She had slipped on a white summer linen dress. He had rarely seen her clothed in anything but black fabric from head to toe before. It made her look so much younger and, briefly, Joe remembered Lily. Where was she now? Had she also been an angel? One of those many kisses had made him think of her. The way that particular young woman had once touched him with a form of reverence, the gentleness with which her lips had roamed over other parts of his body, public and private ones alike, with no shame and even a streak of impudence.

Alraune drew the curtains open. The magic light flooded in and Joe had to squint.

"Come," she ordered.

He pushed the sheets aside and stepped out of the bed. He was naked. The way he always slept. He was about to turn round and pick up his clothes from the chair he had left them hanging on, but Alraune denied him. "Stay as you are," she said. "There will be no one in the streets watching."

Joe caught sight of himself in the mirror. His hair was all over the place, curling at the back out of control, irregular in length, untidy; his cock dangled uselessly between his legs, at rest, just a minor landmark below his stomach; he was overweight but not obese; his chest was hairy and his legs long and steady.

She led him to the door.

Outside, the sun was now setting and a dozen angels similarly dressed in white linen garbs awaited. Alraune took the zigzagging path that led to the edge of town and Joe followed, self-conscious because of his nudity although, as she had predicted, none of the inhabitants of the town were present, let alone watching. He obediently followed her and the troop of angels, all in identical uniforms of sort, stepped into line behind him, forming a most curious procession. Joe was a cauldron of contradicting emotions: slightly aroused at being naked amongst thirteen clothed women, but also experiencing a sense of the ridiculous at how actually unerotic the situation was, or was going to be. A thin smile appeared on his lips as he thought back to Christ's calvary walk and considered the analogy so totally absurd. He had never had much truck with religion and Bible stories.

The file made its way to the edge of town where the woods – you couldn't properly call it a forest yet – stood.

This where the gallows had been installed, just on the edge of the trees. Below it, the earth had been dug up and the mandrake root buried just below the surface.

Alraune led Joe to the rope and wrapped the noose around his neck. "It won't hurt," she whispered.

There was no time for last words or posturing.

Just a naked old man buffeted by an innocent breeze, exposed, helpless, resigned.

The wooden stool was shoved aside and Joe dropped into the gaping void separating his bare feet from the ground.

He had no torrent of visions or the grace of seeing his life unfold before his eyes, the violence of the fall broke his neck instantly and he was dead within seconds as his dangling body still went through obscene tremors and, as planned by the angels, all in the bat of an eyelid his penis rose and grew in tumescence and discharged a thin stream of ejaculate which fell to the ground below. It only took a few seconds.

It would take a few weeks before the angels would discover if he had properly fertilised the mandrake root and given birth to another future tree.

Should it grow in size and transcend its incarnation as a mere root it would henceforth be known as Joseph's tree. And he would become a part of the forest, as had before him Hans-Heinz, Patrick, Foster, Vernon, Pierre, Scott, Serge, Cesare, Lenny and three handful of other men, each of whose offered seed had successfully mated with the mandrake root and given birth to a new tree. It would be several generations before anyone would even know whether the newly-created trees of the Exopotamia forest would possess any particular powers, but that's another story.

The Ways of the Untold Tales

My name is Lily.

I once worked as a waitress in Newfoundland and Labrador.

I now live in the Garden District of New Orleans, in an old plantation house full of carved Jacaranda wood furniture. I shall spare you the tale of how I came to find myself here, who I might be living with and other mundane details. They are irrelevant to this book.

I met a man. He was a dreamer too and he somehow changed my life. He took me to Venice. Odd things happened. I left him. We met again in Paris some time later. None of it was planned. By me at any rate. I've always strongly believed in the way the winds of fate ebb and flow, and how they bring people together and then, on a whim, tear them apart. He took me to a strange bookstore and introduced me to the mysteries of books. Books written, books unwritten, impossible books, pages from which the words jumped out at me, like a mirror to my life, my past, my future.

I am the author of this book. It is about him. Spoiler alert: I have never been to Exopotamia. There is no such place as Exopotomia, but there is a forest somewhere there where each tree has been grown from the seed of dead men. I am sworn by the Fellowship of the Angels to never reveal its exact location. It's not one of the many wonders of the world, nor will it ever be a Unesco heritage site; it's just a forest and to the untrained eye looks just like any other forest.

He once wrote a story in which I appeared as a character, so I felt entitled to do the same.

He had crazy thoughts lurking behind his sadness. I think he was born sad.

His name was Joseph, but everyone called him Joe. Which he disliked.

Once upon a time in Rome I met Ilaria Palomba. It was a lovely name. In Italian it means a female wood pigeon. So much more glamorous than Lily Smith, isn't it? She was downright beautiful. Blonde, dark eye-liner acting as fierce ramparts for her eyes, always dressed in black, pale-skinned, like a silent movie vamp, both mysterious and of the flesh succulent. So unlike us pasty, short, waif-like creatures from the far North. She was a poet but wanted to be a philosopher. I found her deeply fascinating. When she was in her 20s, as I found out when I researched her online, she had for a brief period performed body art, dancing naked at artistic happenings, allowing others of her persuasion to paint in broad strokes across her body, until she was a canvas, an illustrated women caressed by moving lights where the colours daubed over her flesh melted in a cacophony of sensuality with every movement she made to the beat of the music. I wouldn't have called it art – all a bit pretentious if you ask me – but neither was it mere stripping. She had a great body too; tits I could have killed for (unnecessary information: mine are rather modest…).

Her principal flaw, if it could be considered such, was the fact she had awful taste in men and somehow was unable to make her relationships endure. She worshipped men, always hoping the next one would be the one whose soul would match hers in its depth. They should all have been the ones worshipping her. Maybe the fact was that too many men could not cope with intelligence in a woman, seeing it as a challenge, a cliché; she knew, but also an unavoidable fact of life. But that didn't make the matter any less valid. Following a forlorn succession of ill-fated affairs, mostly with older men, she married. It didn't work out and, following her divorce, prey to despair she jumped out of a fourth storey window, a year or so later.

Ilaria survived, although she badly injured her spine and broke an assortment of bones. Following months of operations and intense physiotherapy, she still had difficulty walking and was constantly fighting the pain that had now taken a permanent hold of her body. Maybe Ilaria had thought she could fly and become an angel?

What a fucking waste!

Joe always told me everyone has stories to tell, and I was tempted to write a book about Ilaria. I wanted to call it 'The Philosopher Who Thought She Could Fly' but vestigial decency held me back. She was still alive, after all, and there was so much I didn't know about her that attempting such a book would have been a form of betrayal. There is solidarity between women. Not that Joe would have had such qualms. All his books featured women he had known, and variations thereof. He was a man who loved women, imperfect, delusional at times, but writing about them was also a form of homage, it kept him alive. Until he reached Exopotomia.

I was briefly tempted to bring the books he had spied on the shelf at *Il Sogno* to life.

Surely, they begged to be written, rescued from the limbo where they lay in stasis?

Would the Rabbi from Tallinn sculpt a golem into reality from the dark amber he would use as raw material?

Should the girl from the Australian gold mine walk out into a hurricane, strip off her clothes and dance like a dervish in the storm?

Would I reveal that the Jew from Constantinople was actually the Wandering Jew in his 21st century manifestation?

Was the Mage of New Orleans just a disguise for the bookseller of Cannaregio, with his disappearing store a vortex of unexplainable mysteries?

And I had characters of my own – or had Joe mentioned them to me in passing and my imagination had since appropriated their imaginary identity? The violin player who played as a prelude to sex; the archipelago hunter; the young American woman who would allow men to do anything they wanted to her except touch her breasts... All characters in search of a story.

But then, I decided, these were books which others could write better than I ever could and didn't they say you should write about what you know? And I knew about Joe.

So, this is the book that I wrote.

You could call it a short novel; you can call it anything you want.

Joe's book; I'm just an unimportant, minor character; as it should be.

This one's for you, Joe. May the forest treat you well.

Also from BLACK SHUCK *Signature*

THE THREE BOOKS
by
Paul StJohn Mackintosh

"I've been told that this is the most elegant thing I've ever written. I can't think how such a dark brew of motifs came together to create that effect. But there's unassuaged longing and nostalgia in here, interwoven with the horror, as well as an unflagging drive towards the final consummation. I still feel more for the story's characters, whether love or loathing, than for any others I've created to date. Tragedy, urban legend, Gothic romance, warped fairy tale of New York: it's all there. And of course, most important of all is the seductive allure of writing and of books – and what that can lead some people to do.

You may not like my answer to the mystery of the third book. But I hope you stay to find out."

Paul StJohn Mackintosh

"Paul StJohn Mackintosh is one of those writers who just seems to quietly get on with the business of producing great fiction... it's an excellent showcase for his obvious talents. His writing, his imagination, his ability to lay out a well-paced and intricate story in only 100 pages is a great testament to his skills."

—This is Horror

blackshuckbooks.co.uk/signature

Also from BLACK SHUCK *Signature*

BLACK STAR, BLACK SUN
by
Rich Hawkins

"Black Star, Black Sun *is my tribute to Lovecraft, Ramsey Campbell, and the haunted fields of Somerset, where I seemed to spend much of my childhood. It's a story about going home and finding horror there when something beyond human understanding begins to invade our reality. It encompasses broken dreams, old memories, lost loved ones and a fundamentally hostile universe. It's the last song of a dying world before it falls to the Black Star.*"

Rich Hawkins

"Black Star, Black Sun *possesses a horror energy of sufficient intensity to make readers sit up straight. A descriptive force that shifts from the raw to the nuanced. A ferocious work of macabre imagination and one for readers of Conrad Williams and Gary McMahon.*"
—Adam Nevill, author of *The Ritual*

"*Reading Hawkins' novella is like sitting in front of a guttering open fire. Its glimmerings captivate, hissing with irrepressible life, and then, just when you're most seduced by its warmth, it spits stinging embers your way. This is incendiary fiction. Read at arms' length.*"
—Gary Fry, author of *Conjure House*

blackshuckbooks.co.uk/signature

Also from BLACK SHUCK Signature

DEAD LEAVES

by

Andrew David Barker

"This book is my love letter to the horror genre. It is about what it means to be a horror fan; about how the genre can nurture an adolescent mind; how it can be a positive force in life.

This book is set during a time when horror films were vilified in the press and in parliament like never before. It is about how being a fan of so-called 'video nasties' made you, in the eyes of the nation, a freak, a weirdo, or worse, someone who could actually be a danger to society.

This book is partly autobiographical, set in a time when Britain seemed to be a war with itself. It is a working class story about hope. All writers, filmmakers, musicians, painters – artists of any kind – were first inspired to create their own work by the guiding light of another's. The first spark that sets them on their way.

This book is about that spark."

Andrew David Barker

"Whilst Thatcher colluded with the tabloids to distract the public... an urban quest for the ultimate video nasty was unfolding, before the forces of media madness and power drunk politicians destroyed the Holy Grail of gore!"

—Graham Humphreys, painter of *The Evil Dead* poster

blackshuckbooks.co.uk/signature

Also from BLACK SHUCK *Signature*

THE FINITE
by
Kit Power

"*The Finite started as a dream; an image, really, on the edge of waking. My daughter and I, joining a stream of people walking past our house. We were marching together, and I saw that many of those behind us were sick, and struggling, and then I looked to the horizon and saw the mushroom cloud. I remember a wave of perfect horror and despair washing over me; the sure and certain knowledge that our march was doomed, as were we.*

The image didn't make it into the story, but the feeling did. King instructs us to write about what scares us. In The Finite, *I wrote about the worst thing I can imagine; my own childhood nightmare, resurrected and visited on my kid.*"

Kit Power

"The Finite *is* Where the Wind Blows *or* Threads *for the 21st century, played out on a tight scale by a father and his young daughter, which only serves to make it all the more heartbreaking.*"

—Priya Sharma, author of *Ormeshadow*

blackshuckbooks.co.uk/signature

Also from BLACK SHUCK *Signature*

RICOCHET

by

Tim Dry

"*With* Ricochet *I wanted to break away from the traditional linear form of storytelling in a novella and instead create a series of seemingly unrelated vignettes. Like the inconsistent chaos of vivid dreams I chose to create stand-alone episodes that vary from being fearful to blackly humorous to the downright bizarre. It's a book that you can dip into at any point but there is an underlying cadence that will carry you along, albeit in a strangely seductive new way.*

Prepare to encounter a diverse collection of characters. Amongst them are gangsters, dead rock stars, psychics, comic strip heroes and villains, asylum inmates, UFOs, occult nazis, parisian ghosts, decaying and depraved royalty and topping the bill a special guest appearance by the Devil himself."

Tim Dry

Reads like the exquisite lovechild of William Burroughs and Philip K. Dick's fiction, with some Ballard thrown in for good measure. Wonderfully imaginative, darkly satirical - this is a must read!

—Paul Kane, author of *Sleeper(s)* and *Ghosts*

blackshuckbooks.co.uk/signature

Also from BLACK SHUCK *Signature*

ROTH-STEYR

by

Simon Bestwick

"You never know which ideas will stick in your mind, let alone where they'll go. Roth-Steyr began with an interest in the odd designs and names of early automatic pistols, and the decision to use one of them as a story title. What started out as an oddball short piece became a much longer and darker tale about how easily a familiar world can fall apart, how old convictions vanish or change, and why no one should want to live forever.

It's also about my obsession with history, in particular the chaotic upheavals that plagued the first half of the twentieth century and that are waking up again. Another 'long dark night of the European soul' feels very close today.

So here's the story of Valerie Varden. And her Roth-Steyr."

Simon Bestwick

"A slice of pitch-black cosmic pulp, elegant and inventive in all the most emotionally engaging ways."

—Gemma Files, author of *In That Endlessness, Our End*

blackshuckbooks.co.uk/signature

Also from BLACK SHUCK *Signature*

A DIFFERENT KIND OF LIGHT

by

Simon Bestwick

"When I first read about the Le Mans Disaster, over twenty years ago, I knew there was a story to tell about the newsreel footage of the aftermath – footage so appalling it was never released. A story about how many of us want to see things we aren't supposed to, even when we insist we don't.

What I didn't know was who would tell that story. Last year I finally realised: two lovers who weren't lovers, in a world that was falling apart. So at long last I wrote their story and followed them into a shadow land of old films, grief, obsession and things worse than death.

You only need open this book, and the film will start to play."

Simon Bestwick

"Compulsively readable, original and chilling. Simon Bestwick's witty, engaging tone effortlessly and brilliantly amplifies its edge-of-your-seat atmosphere of creeping dread. I'll be sleeping with the lights on."

—Sarah Lotz, author of *The Three, Day Four, The White Road* & *Missing Person*

blackshuckbooks.co.uk/signature

Also from BLACK SHUCK *Signature*

THE INCARNATIONS OF MARIELA PEÑA
by
Steven J Dines

"The Incarnations of Mariela Peña *is unlike anything I have ever written. It started life (pardon the pun) as a zombie tale and very quickly became something else: a story about love and the fictions we tell ourselves.*

During its writing, I felt the ghost of Charles Bukowski looking over my shoulder. I made the conscious decision to not censor either the characters or myself but to write freely and with brutal, sometimes uncomfortable, honesty. I was betrayed by someone I cared deeply for, and like Poet, I had to tell the story, or at least this incarnation of it. A story about how the past refuses to die."

Steven J Dines

"*Call it literary horror, call it psychological horror, call it a journey into the darkness of the soul. It's all here. As intense and compelling a piece of work as I've read in many a year.*"

—Paul Finch, author of *Kiss of Death* and *Stolen*, and editor of the *Terror Tales* series.

blackshuckbooks.co.uk/signature

Also from BLACK SHUCK Signature

THE DERELICT
by
Neil Williams

"The Derelict *is really a story of two derelicts – the events on the first and their part in the creation of the second.*

With this story I've pretty much nailed my colours to the mast, so to speak. As the tale is intended as a tribute to stories by the likes of William Hope Hodgson or H P Lovecraft (with a passing nod to Coleridge's Ancient Mariner), where some terrible event is related in an unearthed journal or (as is the case here) by a narrator driven to near madness.

The primary influence on the story was the voyage of the Demeter, from Bram Stoker's Dracula, *one of the more compelling episodes of that novel. Here the crew are irrevocably doomed from the moment they set sail. There is never any hope of escape or salvation once the nature of their cargo becomes apparent. This was to be my jumping off point with* The Derelict.

Though I have charted a very different course from the one taken by Stoker, I have tried to remain resolutely true to the spirit of that genre of fiction and the time in which it was set."

Neil Williams

"Fans of supernatural terror at sea will love The Derelict. *I certainly did."*

—Stephen Laws, author of *Ferocity* and *Chasm*

blackshuckbooks.co.uk/signature

Also from BLACK SHUCK *Signature*

AND THE NIGHT DID CLAIM THEM

by

Duncan P Bradshaw

"*The night is a place where the places and people we see during the day are changed. Their properties — especially how we interact and consider them — are altered. But more than that, the night changes us as people. It's a time of day which both hides us away in the shadows and opens us up for reflection. Where we peer up at the stars, made aware of our utter insignificance and wonder, 'what if?' This book takes something that links every single one of us, and tries to illuminate its murky depths, finding things both familiar and alien. It's a story of loss, hope, and redemption; a barely audible whisper within, that even in our darkest hour, there is the promise of the light again.*"

Duncan P Bradshaw

"*A creepy, absorbing novella about loss, regret, and the blackness awaiting us all. Bleak as hell; dark and silky as a pint of Guinness - I loved it.*"

—James Everington, author of *Trying To Be So Quiet* and *The Quarantined City*

blackshuckbooks.co.uk/signature

Also from BLACK SHUCK *Signature*

AZEMAN
OR, THE TESTAMENT OF QUINCEY MORRIS

by

Lisa Moore

"How much do we really know about Quincey Morris?

In one of the greatest Grand-Guignol moments of all time, Dracula is caught feeding Mina blood from his own breast while her husband lies helpless on the same bed. In the chaos that follows, Morris runs outside, ostensibly in pursuit. "I could see Quincey Morris run across the lawn," Dr. Seward says, "and hide himself in the shadow of a great yew-tree. It puzzled me to think why he was doing this..." Then the doctor is distracted, and we never do find out.

This story rose up from that one question: Why, in this calamitous moment, did the brave and stalwart Quincey Morris hide behind a tree?"

Lisa Moore

"A fresh new take on one of the many enigmas of Dracula – just what is Quincey Morris's story?"

—Kim Newman, author of the *Anno Dracula* series

blackshuckbooks.co.uk/signature

Also from BLACK SHUCK *Signature*

SHADE OF STILLTHORPE
by
Tim Major

"It's fair to say that parenthood has dominated my thoughts — and certainly my identity — for the last nine years. While I love my children unconditionally, I'm morbidly fascinated by the idea of parenthood lacking an instinctive bond to counter the difficulties and sacrifices of such a period of life. And I'm afraid of any possible future in which that bond might be weaker.

Identity is a slippery thing. More than anything, I'm scared of losing it — my own, and those of the people I love. Several of my novels and stories have related to this fear. In Shade of Stillthorpe, it's quite literal: how would you react if your child was unrecognisable, suddenly, in all respects?"

Tim Major

A seemingly impossible premise becomes increasingly real in this inventive and heartbreaking tale of loss."

—Lucie McKnight Hardy, author of *Dead Relatives*

"Parenthood is a forest of emotions, including jealousy, confusion and terror, in Shade of Stillthorpe. It's a dark mystery that resonated deeply with me."
—Aliya Whiteley, author of *The Loosening Skin*

blackshuckbooks.co.uk/signature

Also from BLACK SHUCK Signature

SORROWMOUTH
by
Simon Avery

"For a long time Sorrowmouth existed as three or four separate ideas in different notebooks until one day, in a flash of divine inspiration, I recognised the common ground they shared with each other. A man trekking from one roadside memorial to another, in pursuit of grief; Beachy Head and its long dark history of suicide; William Blake and his angelic visions on Peckham Rye; Blake again with The Ghost of a Flea; a monstrous companion, bound by lifes' cruelty...

As I wrote I discovered these disparate elements were really about me getting to some deeper truth about myself, and about all the people I've known in my life, about the struggles we all have that no one save for loved ones see – alcoholism, dependence, self doubt, grief, mental illness. Sorrowmouth is about the mystery hiding at the heart of all things, making connections in the depths of sorrow, and what you have to sacrifice for a moment of vertigo."

Simon Avery

"Sorrowmouth is a story for these dark days. Simon Avery summons the spirit of William Blake in this visionary exploration of the manifestations of our grief and pain."
—Priya Sharma, author of *Ormeshadow*

blackshuckbooks.co.uk/signature

Also from BLACK SHUCK *Signature*

THE DREAD THEY LEFT BEHIND

by

Gary Fry

"The seed of this novella was a single image I'd long had in mind before composition. A young boy standing in a farmyard no longer knowing which hand he led with. That struck me as a promising metaphor for something my conscious mind had yet to catch up with, and indeed it was another few years before I finally figured it all out. By this time I'd returned to my early love of the classic dark novella. Lovecraft, obviously, but also a renewed appreciation of Arthur Machen, particularly his criminally underrated 'The Terror'. In that piece, I was struck by its accumulative, almost investigative structure, the way it drew upon different sources of information to conjure a vision packed with verisimilitude.

In The Dread They Left Behind, I wanted to evoke an isolated rural community via the medium of a retrospective first-person narrator along the lines of he who regales us in HPL's 'The Color out of Space'. The difference is that mine is directly exposed to and physically affected by the historical events. Along with all the requisite intrigue and frights, the piece allowed me to explore concerns I have about political extremism. It took a long while to get right -- I tinkered with it for years. But for me it embodies everything I hold dear in the field. Whether it does so successfully, I leave for readers to determine."

Gary Fry

blackshuckbooks.co.uk/signature

Also from BLACK SHUCK *Signature*

JAEGER
by
Simon Bestwick

"Roth-Steyr, *the story of Valerie Varden, (or to use her full name, Countess Valerie Elisabeth Franzsiska von Bradenstein-Vršovci, reluctant immortal and former assassin of the Habsburg Empire,) wasn't quite like anything I'd written before. And almost as soon as I'd finished it, I knew Val had more to say. So I picked up her trail again, and found her making her way across a darkening Europe, hunted by a shadowy foe. Someone wants her dead: to find out who Val will need to remember everything she tried to forget. She must become, once more, an assassin. A killer. A Jaeger.*"

Simon Bestwick

blackshuckbooks.co.uk/signature

Also from BLACK SHUCK *Signature*

CHARLIE SAYS
by
Neil Williamson

"I don't know anyone who grew up in the 1970s who wasn't scarred by the public information safety films on British TV. Those tiny, doom-filled dramas slipped in between the cartoons were often only fifteen or thirty seconds long but, by God, they caught our attention. Don't play with matches, or old fridges. Or kites or frisbees, should you happen to be near a pylon or electricity substation. Be careful crossing the road and running along the beach. And also near ponds and lakes, or when swimming in the sea. And never, ever talk to strangers.

And then, of course, there was Protect and Survive. A full set of instructions for what to do in the event of nuclear war. Coming from a time of such existential dread, is it any wonder that those films are now considered a cornerstone of the UK's collective Horror imagination?

I'd wanted to use them in a story for a long time, but the idea lay dormant until I realized two things. Firstly, that there was an element of warding ritual and incantation to them ("Look left, look right...", "Charley says...") reminiscent of folk horror, only in the urban environment rather than the usual remote rural setting. And, secondly, that those films were what Britain was scared of fifty years ago. What I ought to be writing about was what really terrifies me about this country now.*"*

Neil Williamson

blackshuckbooks.co.uk/signature

Milton Keynes UK
Ingram Content Group UK Ltd.
UKHW022223230824
447237UK00005B/16